AWARDS FOR AIDAN CHAMBERS

Michael L. Printz Award
Hans Christian Andersen Award
Carnegie Medal
Italian Andersen Award
Dutch Silver Pencil
Eleanor Farjeon Award

AWARDS AND PRAISE FOR *DYING TO KNOW YOU*

Cooperative Children's Book Center (CCBC) Choices 2013—Young
Adult Fiction

★ "Deliberate in pace and carefully insightful in its investigation of character,
Chamber's latest is a work of art that repays multiple readings."
—*Booklist*, starred review

★ "Chambers delivers yet another intellectually satisfying novel
with equal parts philosophy and repartee, and this one may
have broader teen appeal than his most recent efforts."
—*The Horn Book*, starred review

★ "Packed to the brim with challenging ideas, the latest from Chambers—winner
of the Printz Award, Carnegie Medal, and Hans Christian Andersen Award,
among others—is simultaneously an acutely observed (and surprising) love
story; the chronicle of a young man coming into his own as an artist; and a
slippery, twisting examination of the art of storytelling."
—*Publishers Weekly*, starred review

★ "Readers are hooked with snappy dialogue and keen insights; Karl is a
multifaceted and likable character who will keep them engaged and
rooting for him to find his way in love and in life."
—*School Library Journal*, starred review

"This quietly understated performance captures the wistfulness of music in a
minor key and is ultimately successful in its life-affirming message."
—*Kirkus Reviews*

AIDAN CHAMBERS

DYING TO KNOW YOU

AMULET BOOKS
NEW YORK

The Library of Congress has catalogued the hardcover edition of this book as follows:

Chambers, Aidan.
Dying to know you / Aidan Chambers.
pages cm
Summary: Struggling through his dyslexia to try to fulfill his girlfriend Fiorella's request for a letter revealing his secret self, eighteen-year-old Karl asks Fiorella's favorite author for help, and he agrees only if Karl will submit to a series of interviews, which prove helpful to both men.
ISBN 978-1-4197-0165-8 (hardback)
[1. Self perception—Fiction. 2. Authors—Fiction. 3. Interpersonal relations—Fiction. 4. Dyslexia—Fiction.] I. Title.
PZ7.C3557Dyi2012
[Fic]—dc23
2012000843

Paperback ISBN: 978-1-4197-0794-0

ABRAMS
THE ART OF BOOKS SINCE 1949
115 West 18th Street
New York, NY 10011
www.abramsbooks.com

TO SUSAN VAN METRE

DYING TO KNOW YOU

one

- - - - - - -

"COULD I TALK TO YOU?"

"Why?"

"You're a writer?"

"And?"

"I need your help."

"You see the sign on the door?"

"Yes."

"What does it say?"

"No visitors without appointment."

"Have you an appointment?"

"No."

"Then I suggest you make one."

"Could I make an appointment?"

"When for?"

"Now."

I couldn't help laughing. Anyway, there was something about him, an indefinable quality that instantly appealed.

"What sort of help do you want?"

"With my girlfriend."

"I don't know anything about you, never mind your girlfriend."

"I can explain."

"Young man. I'm seventy-five. Happily married for over forty years. What would I know about girls these days?"

"You write about them."

"You've read my books?"

"No."

"So how do you know?"

"My girlfriend told me. She's a fan. And I looked you up on the internet."

"Really? Well, at least you're honest. But in any case, the girls in my books are fictions. I made them up. They don't have minds of their own. Real girls do."

"The help is just for me, really. Not my girlfriend."

"Look, if we're going to continue this conversation, which it seems we are, you'd better come inside."

Rooms are a fixed size, which can't be altered without pulling down walls and building new ones. They should be unchanging in shape and proportions. But sometimes they do change depending on who's in them.

I led him into the sitting room. He was tall, well built

but not bulky, not overbearing. I was surprised, because the room didn't shrink as it usually did when visitors came in. It got larger.

When we'd sat down, he on the edge of the sofa, leaning forward, elbows on knees, eyes looking at his hands clasped as if in prayer, me in the armchair facing him, I asked again how he thought I could help.

"My girlfriend wants me to write about myself," he said.

"And?"

"About myself. Inside."

"What? You mean your feelings?"

"My inner secrets, she said."

"Why?"

"She quoted something at me."

"Can you remember it?"

"'How can you call them friends when they do not know their mutual feelings.'"

"That's good. Did she say who said it?"

"Aristotle."

"Aristotle? She's read Aristotle?"

"No idea."

"Maybe she picked it up from the internet."

"She does read a lot. She'd like it here," he added, looking at the shelves of books.

"How old?"

"Seventeen."

"She's some girl, if she's read Aristotle."

"Well, yes, she is."

"Or maybe she's just good at finding quotes." I let that sink in before I said, "So what do you want me to do?"

"Help me write the stuff she wants."

"Why can't you write it yourself?"

"Hate writing."

"Then don't."

"She says she'll only go on with me if I do. She's made a list of questions she wants me to answer. And I have to do it in what she calls full-dress English."

"'Full-dress'?"

"Yes. Proper punctuation, spelling and stuff. And printed out. I hate doing that. It's torture."

"Not that bad, surely?"

"Yes, it is. And, anyway, I don't know what to write."

"What do you want me to do, then? Make it up?"

"No! . . . But that wouldn't be such a bad idea, come to think of it."

He looked at me and smiled for the first time and said, "Only joking. But still . . ."

"Still what?"

"Dunno . . . Well, I do, to be honest. There's a problem."

"Which is?"

He examined his hands again, fiddled with his fingers, took in a breath, and gave me a defiant look.

"I'm dyslexic."

"Ah!" I said. "I see."

Defiance turned to apology. "I have trouble writing. Not reading so much. But writing. Things get jumbled.

Not just letters and words. The sentences and the thoughts as well. Something happens between what's in my head and what comes out when I try to write it down. It's torture."

"Your parents know about this, and your teachers, of course?"

"My parents, and the teachers did when I was at school."

"You're not at school?"

"No."

"How old are you?"

"Eighteen."

I'd have said sixteen.

"What do you do for a living?"

"I'm training to be a plumber."

"I see. What's your name, by the way?"

"Karl. Karl Williamson."

"Haven't I seen you around?"

"We did some work in a house up the road not long ago. I used to go past your house. You were in the garden a couple of times."

"I thought I'd seen you. And your girlfriend, what's her name?"

"Fiorella. Fiorella Seabourne."

"Fiorella. Unusual name."

"Italian. Her mother's Italian."

"And she understands? About your dyslexia."

"She doesn't know."

"You haven't told her?"

"No."

"Then tell her."

"Not yet."

"Why not?"

"Don't want to."

"That's not good enough. If I'm going to help, you have to level with me."

He sat back, deciding, I think, whether he wanted to go on with this, after all. Then:

"Like I said, she's a big reader. And a big writer as well. Always at it. She wrote to you once. An email."

"Really? Did I answer?"

"Yes."

"You've read it?"

"No. Fiorella told me about it. She said she asked about being a writer and you told her that real writers read a lot of the best stuff ever written and write something every day, it doesn't matter what. You said writing a book was the most difficult thing you had ever tried to do and told her to do something else unless she was passionate about it."

"Did I? I can only say, if I did, I am in complete agreement with myself."

He laughed.

Karl was no glamour boy. But even during this first meeting I discovered he had something better. The kind of intelligence that's more attractive than physical beauty.

"Let me guess," I said. "You're afraid Fiorella will give up on you if she finds out you're dyslexic, because she'll think you're stupid."

"Something like that."

"In which case, why bother? She's not worthy of you."

He ignored the criticism and the compliment. I'm always interested in what people ignore in a conversation, especially when talking about their problems. The question is: Did they take in what was being said? Or didn't they want to hear it? This time, Karl's eyes shifted from mine, and looked down at his hands, now clenched between his knees.

"So why don't you tell Fiorella about it?"

"I don't want to tell her till she knows me better."

"How long have you been seeing each other?"

"Three months."

"Not long."

"Long enough."

"Long enough for what?"

"For me to know I want to hang on to her."

I let that pass. I knew exactly what he meant.

"She'll be bound to find out sometime. What then?"

"Dunno. I'll deal with it when it happens."

Not wise. But I needed time to think it over.

"What do you do in your spare time?" I asked.

"Fish. Play rugby. Play chess. Cook."

"So," I said, "you like facts and doing practical things, but aren't too keen on talking about your feelings."

"Something like that."

"OK. Let me sum up and you can tell me if I've got it right. You've met a girl you admire and would like to keep her as your girlfriend. She fancies you and she wants to know about your private life, your intimate self, because she believes that real friends—let's say, lovers— tell each other about their secret selves. And she insists on you writing this. But you don't even like talking about yourself, and writing would be torture because of your dyslexia. So you've come to me, who you know nothing about except that I write books Fiorella likes. And you want me to help you by writing for you what she wants you to write for her in proper English. Is that it?"

"That's about it, yes."

"Good. Which leaves us with a couple of questions. One: Why should I help you? And two: If I help you, what is it you want me to write, exactly?"

"I don't know."

"You don't know what?"

"The answer to both questions."

I laughed.

"You must be desperate."

Karl laughed too. "I am!"

There was one of those pauses when neither can think what to say next. In the silence, an intuitive shift, felt rather than thought, occurs in knowledge of the other.

Karl looked awkward. In the silence, this moment of sudden awkwardness was like a door opening just enough to allow a glimpse into a room meant to be kept secret. I saw that what it kept hidden was shyness and that Karl's brusqueness was a front, a carapace against discovery.

I knew this was true because it was like looking at myself.

And this, combined with the attraction of his intelligence, gave me the answer to one of the two questions that Karl couldn't answer. Why should I help him?

Because helping him was like helping myself when I was his age and helping myself with my own difficulties now.

I wondered what Karl was thinking of me.

"How about a coffee?" I said, to break the impasse. "Or something else?"

"If you like," he said, torn, I guessed, between the impulse to cut and run and his overriding need to obtain what he'd come for.

I led him to the kitchen.

Rooms change their shape according to who is in them, and there are rooms in which you feel more comfortable than in others.

For me, there are two. My workroom, the only place where, when I am alone, I am entirely myself, and because of this is a sacred room where I take very few people. And the kitchen—another workroom, now that I think of it— where I can be at ease when talking to visitors.

Karl sat at the table while I made coffee, asking him no more than the ritual how strong, with milk or without, sugar or not, and would he like a biscuit? I was pleased to see that he visibly relaxed. Another kitchen man, perhaps?

"You say you cook?" I asked as I gave him a mug of coffee and a chocolate ginger biscuit.

"Yes," he said. "You?"

"It relaxes me after a day's work. People think writing is what my father used to call head work. And it is, partly. But it's gut work as well. You live in your guts everything that happens in the story. Or at least I do. After a day of it my guts are tied in knots. Cooking helps to undo them. Who taught you?"

"School. Took it as an option."

"Lucky you. Boys weren't given the option in my day. What do you like most about it?"

"You don't have to write anything."

We laughed.

"And," he went on, "it's useful. You're making something people need and they like. Or they do if you get it right and do it well."

"You like getting things right and doing them well?"

He gave me a shy glance.

"Don't you?"

"Yes. And you know what I like about cooking? The tools. You don't use many tools as a writer. Pencils, pens, paper. A computer, of course, though I never think of it as a tool, only as a machine. My father was a joiner. Very skilled woodworker. He had lots of tools. I loved to watch him use them. All sorts of hammers, chisels, saws, awls, screwdrivers. He had some special knives. He had drills and clamps and punches and files. All of them with their own places to be, hanging on the wall in front of his bench or in his toolboxes. Planes, for instance, rasps, pliers, spanners, a set square, rulers. Lovely. All of them a bit worn and shiny from use. I thought they were beautiful. Still do. Not to mention the wonderful smell of wood. Well, cooking is a bit like that. Plenty of attractive tools to play with, and, as you say, something useful to make with them."

He nodded.

"Sorry," I said. "Carried away by nostalgia."

"Copper pans," he said with a grin. "I have a thing about copper pans."

"I can see why."

"I've a couple of saucepans, an omelette pan, and a copper bowl. I'd quite like some gratin dishes. Did you know that copper was the first metal used for making tools? That's because you can find it naturally, in the ground. It doesn't have to be made like iron or steel. It's the only metal that's like that."

"Really? I didn't know."

"And it's good for cooking because copper heats up quicker than any other metal used for cooking, and it heats up evenly all over the surface. The best pots are thick and heavy. Which is nice as well."

"They look lovely too, don't they? A beautiful colour, and shiny."

"But you have to polish them to keep them shiny. We use a lot of copper pipe in plumbing. I like bending it and soldering the joins."

He became aware of himself and shrugged.

We smiled at each other and were silent.

Another shift had happened.

I was beginning to see what Fiorella might see in him.

"Getting back to Fiorella," I said after a while.

He frowned.

"Have you written anything to her? You said she gave you some questions. Have you answered any of them?"

"Yes. But I tore it up. It was crap."

"Pity. Look, if I'm going to help you, I have to have something to go on. I can't make it up, now can I, seriously?"

"No. I know."

"The best I could do is turn what you've written into proper English—punctuation, grammar, spelling, that sort of thing—and maybe help you with the expression. But if I do more than that, well, we'd both be perpetrating a deception, wouldn't we? A lie."

He nodded.

I could see Fiorella's problem. Getting anything out of him was like squeezing juice from a stone.

I tried another tack.

"How often do you see each other?"

"Once a week mostly. She's studying for exams, and I do quite a lot of overtime. In my job you have to go to people's houses in the evening when they're at home from work. So it's hard for us to meet except at weekends."

"Doesn't live near you?"

"No."

"You have transport?"

"Only a bike. Don't have a license. Keep failing the theory."

"Why? It's not that difficult, is it?"

A blank stare.

"Ah yes. Of course. Sorry!"

I cleared the mugs away, and leaned against the kitchen bench while I thought what to say next. I'd had enough for today.

"I'll tell you what. Why don't you bring Fiorella's questions to me tomorrow? I'll look through them and we'll talk some more. Maybe I can work out what to do when I see what she is asking. How does that sound?"

He took a moment before saying, "OK. What time? I'll be at work till sixish."

"Would eight suit you?"

"OK."

"Eight tomorrow, then, with Fiorella's questions."

He followed me to the front door.

"Thanks," he said, as he went past me. But stopped on the doorstep, and said, "Could I ask you something?"

"Sure."

"Why are you helping me?"

I gave him a wry look.

"Because you asked."

"That's all?"

"Perhaps one good turn deserves another?"

"Tit for tat."

"Quid pro quo."

"You scratch my back and I'll scratch yours."

"Not exactly what I had in mind."

"Don't see how I can help *you*."

"Time will tell."

I waved a salute and closed the door before he could say anything else.

TWO

- - - - - - -

I SEARCHED THROUGH MY FOLDER OF READERS' EMAILS AND FOUND
Fiorella's. Sent the year before, when she said she was sixteen. The passage that caught my eye was this:

> I'm not much of a talker, though I often wish I
> were. So writing is very important to me. It's like
> a sleepover, when you feel you can say all kinds of
> things, because the darkness hides your blushes.
>
> I think there is no better way to get to know
> someone than reading what they write. Even if I
> lived with someone I loved, I'd still want to write
> to him all the time, and him to me.
>
> I don't have a boyfriend at the moment. I have
> only had a few. Three, to be exact. They were all
> pretty useless. None of them was any good at
> writing. I live in hope!

In one of your stories, a girl wrote that she lives to read and writes to live the life she cannot live otherwise. Is that true for you as well? I hadn't thought of it before, but I think it is true for me too.

Some of my friends say I'm a bit weird for reading and writing so much and taking it so seriously. In my opinion, they are the ones who are weird for not taking it seriously. Do you agree?

And do you have any tips that will help me to become a professional writer, because there is nothing else I want to be.

I tried to put myself in Karl's shoes by remembering myself at eighteen, when I was as shy and unrevealing as him, and drafted a letter he might send to Fiorella to keep her happy while he and I worked out what to do about the questions she'd set him.

Dear Fiorella [or Hi, Fiorella, or any salutation you prefer],
    I've read your questions.
    Do you really want to torture me?
    If so, you're going the right way about it.
    Like I told you, writing isn't my favourite thing.
    But you've given me this ultimatum.
    I think you're testing me, to see how much I want you.

Answer: Very much.

So I'll do it. Or I'll try.

But don't expect me to be quick. Answering all your questions could take a book. I have to think what I want to say and I am a slow writer.

I will send you a few answers, maybe just one at a time so you don't have to wait and get tired of waiting and ditch me anyway.

Is that OK?

Love [or whatever valediction you prefer],

Karl

THRee

- - - - - - -

|

Karl arrived on the dot of eight.

"You're prompt."

"Don't like to be late."

"And don't like to be kept waiting."

"No."

"Nor me. A man of the clock."

We smiled agreement.

He was washed and brushed up. Long-sleeved black crewneck sweatshirt, well-fitting jeans, Merrell Urbino shoes, short, jet-black hair gelled into spikes a hedgehog would have been proud of.

He asked for a beer. I didn't have any, as I hate the stuff. So he settled for a glass of red wine. We sat as before in the kitchen. I was glad to see he relaxed at once.

He read my draft letter while I looked through Fiorella's questions, a list of more than fifty on two pages. And a set of six index cards on which Karl had organised the questions into topics, one topic to a card: Likes and Dislikes, Beliefs, Aims and Plans, Fiorella and Me, Love and Sex, Interests and Activities.

I asked him what he thought of the letter.

He gave me an assessing look.

"I'm a writer," I said. "I'm used to people telling me they don't like what I've written. Speak your mind."

He shrugged. "It's all right as a letter."

"But?"

"It's not. Not *me*, if you know what I mean."

"Not the way you'd have expressed it."

He nodded.

"OK. Let's have a go at it later. What about these questions? The answers would fill a book."

"That's what I said."

"And she said?"

"Write a chapter at a time."

"She has high expectations."

"About everything."

"And you like this about her?"

"Yes."

"Like her. Or love her?"

He blushed and frowned at his hands bunched round the glass on the table.

Too soon for such a question.

"Look," I said quickly. "Why don't you tell me how you met?"

He sat back, heaved a sigh like a boy being made to do his homework but knowing there was no way out of it, and pushed himself to begin. "I was on a job with my boss. Putting a new bathroom in a granny flat at Fiorella's house. We were finishing the second fit. Most times we'd been there the granny was around. Both Fiorella's parents have full-time jobs so they're out all day, and Fiorella was at school. But it was her half-term holiday. The granny wanted to go out. Fiorella was told to see we were OK. She wasn't that bothered and kept out of the way."

"But you'd seen her before and liked what you'd seen?"

"Didn't take much notice. She was just a schoolgirl. And she hadn't taken any notice of me. I thought she was a bit stuck-up."

"And this was what? Three months ago?"

"Three months and a week today."

"So what happened next?"

"My boss got an emergency call from one of our regulars. An old lady who lives on her own. He rushed off to deal with her and left me to get on. Which only meant clearing up because we'd nearly finished. He told me to wait till he came back to check everything was OK."

"Let me guess. You cleared up, called for Fiorella to tell her you were finished and Eros struck."

I was glad he felt confident enough to laugh.

"Except it was chess."

"*Chess?*"

"Chess."

"How does chess come into it?"

"She said would I like to wait in the kitchen and have a cup of coffee. I felt a bit embarrassed. I'd seen a chess set when she took me through the living room to the kitchen. I play chess. So for something to say I asked her if she played. She said she did and would I like a game? Do you play?"

"Sorry, no."

"You should. It's a good game."

"I'm not a games player. To my mind, there are enough chances to fail in life without inventing more. But I've always liked the look of the pieces."

"Me too. That's what attracted me at first."

"When was that?"

"My . . . At school, when I was eleven. And another reason I like it"—a wide smile—"you don't have to write anything. And you don't talk while you're playing because you have to concentrate, which was useful that first time with Fiorella."

"Who won?"

"We hadn't finished when my boss came back. It was pretty even between us."

"And you agreed to meet again to finish?"

"Yes."

"Who suggested that?"

"Fiorella."

"So she made the first move."

He smiled. "White always makes the first move."

"She's blonde?"

"Sort of. Strawberry blonde."

"You met again. Where?"

"Her house."

"When?"

"Next day."

"Who won?"

"She did."

"You were nervous?"

"Well, she *is* good."

"What else?"

"What else did we do? Nothing. Talked chess. Played through a famous game just for fun. She has quite a lot of books on chess. Then she suggested some matches, three games a match starting at the weekend."

"So it was chess brought you together and kept you together. What's the score now?"

"Three to two in her favour. And two draws."

"But you must have done other things as well?"

"She watched me play rugby a couple of times. Last two games of the season."

"Who do you play for?"

"Nothing special. Highwood."

"But they're pretty good, aren't they? Always on the local news."

"Not too bad. You follow the game?"

"Sorry! I'm no more a rugby man than a chess man."

"Fiorella's not interested, either. But she likes tennis, so we've started playing that."

"Doing any better than at chess?"

"Two to one in my favour."

"I see one of her questions is why you like rugby so much."

"Tried to explain, but she can't understand it."

"Maybe that's a question we could start with? You know what you want to say. It shouldn't be too difficult."

"If you like."

"OK, let's do it. I'll take some notes while we talk. Then I'll write what you tell me. You can comment and we'll revise to suit you. And when you're happy with it, I'll print it out and you can give it to Fiorella. How about that?"

||

My summary of Karl's answers to my questions about why he likes rugby so much:

I like rugby because it's physical. So are football and hockey. But they aren't physical the same way as rugby. Rugby is a contact sport. I like that. Boxing is as well. But the aim is to hurt your opponent. Rugby can be pretty tough, you might say it's violent at times, but you aren't trying to hurt anybody.

23

It's skilled. You have to use all your skills of the body and the mind. Like chess, you have to think ahead three or four moves. It's a game of strategy and tactics. It's violence used with moral intelligence, if that makes any sense.

It's also fast. It exhausts you. Rugby releases the tensions and pent-up energy that have built up during the week at work. I like leaving a match feeling I've got rid of all the energy that has been locked up inside me. I have to be careful at work, because if I make a mistake it can be a disaster. But in rugby I can let myself go, drive hard, really go for it, and it doesn't matter if I get it wrong, it's only a game. Not that I like getting it wrong. That's not what I'm saying. I'm only saying that I can let myself go while I'm playing.

You can only win at rugby if everyone plays their part and works with the others. People who are only out for themselves, trying to score on their own and be the star, are looked down on. It's a terrific feeling when a move goes totally right, like a combination of passes, or a tackle, or a kick that are spot on. It's as if I'm part of a perfectly functioning machine. It's like music in motion. Almost like dancing. Not that I can dance!

Rugby is a dirty game. I like getting covered in mud and then cleaning it off afterwards. There's something very primitive about it. In fact, now

I come to think of it, there's something very primitive about rugby as a game.

It's so obvious that I won't bother to mention that rugby is good exercise. And it helps to keep me fit.

III

"How's that?"

"OK. It's what I said but tidied up and put into smoother English. Some of the words don't sound like me. And the bit about moral intelligence. I didn't say that."

"Yes, you did, only not in those words, exactly."

"No. They're your words."

"But they say what you mean, don't they?"

"Yes."

"And you can use them yourself now?"

"I suppose."

"So now they're yours as well as mine."

"Are they?"

"You said Fiorella is a strawberry blonde?"

"What's that got to do with it?"

"Did you make it up? Strawberry blonde. Are they your words?"

"No. My mother said that's what she is."

"But you said them to me as if they were yours. You didn't say they are your mother's, did you?"

"No. But . . ."

"And you joked that white always makes the first move. Did you make that up?"

"No! It's a chess rule."

"Which you were taught when you were learning chess. What I'm trying to say is that we've learned everything we say from something or someone else. You've heard of Oscar Wilde?"

"Didn't he write a story called 'The Selfish Giant' or something?"

"He did."

"My dad read it to me when I was little."

"A playwright. Very witty. One day he heard someone make an especially clever joke, and Wilde said to a friend, 'I wish I'd said that.' To which his friend replied, 'You will, Oscar, you will.'"

He laughed. "But I still say 'moral intelligence' isn't the way I talk."

"Well, it is now, Karl, it is now."

"OK, OK! I give in!"

We laughed, and fell suddenly silent, as if somehow it wasn't so funny after all. And I could see from his eyes he'd had enough of me for the day. I'd had enough of me too.

I waved the printout at him.

"You're giving it to Fiorella?"

"Might as well."

"And not give her the first one about answering the questions?"

"No. It's not right and doesn't matter now I've got this one."

"Want to go on with this or not?"

"Yes."

"Any idea when?"

He pondered for a while, eyes on his feet, which I was beginning to know was a habit with him when he was thinking.

"I'm tied up all next week," he said as he folded the printout and put it into the back pocket of his jeans. "Fiorella is away this weekend on a school trip. I thought I'd go trout fishing. There's a stretch of the Wye that's good for trout. I thought I'd try it on Sunday. Trouble is, it'll take most of the day just to get there."

"The Wye isn't that far, surely? An hour's drive, an hour and a half."

"Too far to cycle and have much time there. And with public transport on a Sunday, train and bus, then a bit of a walk, not to mention getting back . . ."

He wasn't hinting, just making a statement of fact.

Now it was my turn to ponder. I knew that if we were to go on meeting, it shouldn't always be at my place. Too restricting and a bit too formal. He was a guest, on his best behaviour. Besides I needed a change, wanted to get out, have some company, and not with old friends who knew me so well the conversation would be predictable and on a topic I wanted to avoid, but with someone who didn't know me and was refreshing.

But how to make a suggestion without having to explain this?

I decided to take a chance and hoped it wouldn't backfire.

By then Karl was ready to go.

"Look," I said. "I had an attack of sciatica recently."

"My boss had that last year. Off work for a few weeks. Very painful, he said."

"Very. I'm on the mend, but it still hurts to drive. I'm OK as a passenger. But driving any distance isn't on. You're a learner driver, I think you said, and must need to practise, so why don't we take my car, you driving?"

"Do you fish?"

"No."

"Won't you be bored? When I'm fishing, I forget the time."

"I'll read. Take a walk. And I like just sitting and looking at the view."

"I don't know."

"You'd be doing me a favour."

"Ah . . . I get it. One good turn."

"Quid pro quo."

"OK. If you're certain."

"I'm certain."

"What if the weather's bad? I'll still fish."

"So the weather's bad."

"You can't drive to the river. You have to walk down some pretty steep tracks through the woods."

"Walking is good for sciatica."

He gave me one of his assessing looks.

I said, "Range Rover Sports SE."

That clinched it.

"Cool! But only if I pay for the petrol."

"Agreed. Think you can handle the Rover?"

"No problem. I'm good at the practical. It's the theory I fail."

"OK," I said. "I'll bring the food. A deal?"

"See you Sunday."

"Would eight o'clock be too early?"

"Earlier if you like. I'm always on the go by seven."

"Seven thirty?"

"I'll be ready."

FOUR

KARL HAD PRINTED OUT FROM THE INTERNET A SET OF LARGE-scale maps, marking with highlighter our journey to the spot on the Wye where he wanted to fish.

Meticulous, neat, well prepared, the pages inserted into the transparent envelopes of a presentation book.

After the maps, a few pages on rainbow trout, the geography, geology and history of the river.

A man after my own heart: preparation, order and information. The job neatly laid out before setting to.

Karl gave me a quick smile:

"Something for you to read if you get bored."

"Good of you to think of it."

"Well, if you don't fish . . . And it's an all-day job."

"I've brought my laptop."

"You're writing a book?"

I wasn't, but didn't want to explain why.

"There's some eBooks on it. I'll not be bored."

"And if it rains?"

"I'll go back to the car."

We drove through Gloucester, over the Severn, and on towards Ross-on-Wye. In silence. Which suited me, as I'm never talkative early in the day, and Karl seemed content to concentrate on his driving, getting used to the Rover, judging speed and distance still not second nature. But I felt safe, the way you do instantly with some drivers, even when they're learning.

It was also a pleasure to be a passenger, able to shift about in my seat to ease the sciatica, and look at the countryside.

Sunday morning early. Very little moving on the road once we were away from the city.

I could sense Karl settling in, and driving with increasing confidence. Loving the car, its power and strength and robust sleekness.

"You said you'd failed the theory part of the driving test?"

"Four times."

"But you don't have to write anything, do you? Isn't it all multiple choice questions or ticks in boxes?"

"There's more to it than that. Didn't score enough marks. So I was failed."

"There was none of that stuff when I did my test. But that was fifty years ago! And you can't take the practical test on the road till you've passed the theory?"

"Right."

"Aren't there theory tests on the internet for practice?"

"Yes."

"Don't you do them?"

"No."

"Why not?"

"Bloody-mindedness."

"What?"

"It's stupid. I don't do them because I know I can pass the test. The trouble is I go to pieces when I know it's a test. I hate tests. I always fail. So I don't do the practice tests because I know I'd pass them easy. They're not a proper test. And the examiner isn't breathing down my neck."

I knew exactly what he meant because I was the same.

I didn't pursue the topic. The irritation in his voice was a warning, and I didn't want to spoil the pleasure of the day.

Silence again for a few miles before Karl said:

"Can I ask you something?"

"Sure."

"You said you've been married over forty years."

I said, "That's right." Adding quickly to avoid more questions, "Did you give Fiorella the letter we wrote?"

He nodded, eyes firmly on the road.

"And?"

"She asked why I wrote about rugby first."

"And you said?"

"Easiest to start with."

"Have you decided what to write about next?"

"I haven't. But Fiorella has."

"Which is?"

"Love."

"*Love!*"

"She wants to know what I think love is."

I couldn't help a burst of laughter.

"Sorry! But she certainly goes for the jugular."

Now Karl laughed.

"What are you going to say?"

"Dunno. Googled it to find out."

This time I managed to keep a straight face.

"Any use?"

"Pages of the stuff. Loads of sections with titles like 'personal love,' and 'interpersonal love,' and 'cultural views,' and 'religious views,' and 'how to love.' It even had one called 'warnings.'"

"Warnings like what?"

"You must love yourself before you can love another. There's always a risk of getting hurt. Don't ask for love and don't force love, and—"

But he couldn't go on because by now we were both bubbling with laughter.

I managed to say, "Not much help, then?"

"About the same as for plumbing a loo."

"How d'you mean?"

"Easier to find out how to do it by doing it than by reading the manual. Every job is different. The instructions are too general. They don't allow for the quirks."

When we'd calmed down, I said, "Must have been a bit of help, though."

"Nar! I mean, I already knew love is supposed to be like it said. A strong emotion. Feeling attached to somebody. Wanting to be with them all the time. But the bit I liked best was where it said it's impossible to define love because it takes so many forms and is so complicated."

"Like plumbing a loo."

"Exactly."

"But," I said, "when you think of all the books there are on the subject, and the thousands, probably millions, of stories there are about love, you'd think we would know everything there is to know."

"Can't say I've read that many."

"No, but still, the fact is, at least this is how it seems to me, everybody has to learn about it from scratch for themselves. And we all make the same mistakes time and again while we're learning."

"Like me learning to read."

"But not when you were learning to plumb a loo."

"No, I was pretty good at that from the off."

"Every man to his last."

"His what?"

"His own trade. The thing he's best at."

"Like you're best at writing?"

"I'm glad you think so."

"Not that I've read anything you've written."

"And I haven't had the pleasure of your plumbing my loo."

"Anytime. You only have to ask."

"Thank you, good sir. Same goes for my books and you reading them."

"One day, one day. Promise."

"And by the way," I said, "as we're talking about plumbing, could you pull over somewhere suitable, at your earliest convenience. My old man's plumbing isn't as efficient as it used to be and my morning coffee is on the way out."

He smiled and after half a mile or so pulled into a lay-by.

There'd been rain in the night. The hedgerow behind which I relieved myself smelt of rotting vegetation and the spoor left by other travellers observing the calls of nature.

When we were on our way again, I said, "What would you like to do about the letter on love to Fiorella? Would you like me to draft something while you're fishing?"

Karl didn't reply at once, then said, "I've been thinking. I know I asked you for help. But it's a bit of a cop-out for me, isn't it?"

I kept quiet, waiting for him to go on.

Which he did after an uncomfortable silence. "Anyway, what I've done is I've written, I mean I've tried to write, well, I have, I've written, it's only a few lines, a try at it, about love, because I think I should give it a go."

"Great!" I said. "That's great, Karl! And you'll send it?"

He glanced at me, the car wobbled, he attended to his driving again, and said, "Yes, but I thought you might have a look at it while I'm fishing, and, you know, tidy it up a bit maybe, or make a few suggestions."

"Be glad to."

"We're nearly there."

"Not far off," I said, checking the map. "Listen to what Mr. William Wordsworth wrote about the place many years ago:

> *And again I hear*
> *These waters, rolling from their mountain-springs*
> *With a soft inland murmur. Once again*
> *Do I behold these steep and lofty cliffs,*
> *That on a wild secluded scene impress*
> *Thoughts of more deep seclusion . . .*
> *O sylvan Wye! thou wanderer thro' the woods*
> *How oft my spirit has turned to thee!*"

"Sounds like he liked it," Karl said.

"He did."

"And sounds like you like that stuff."

"Poetry? I do."

"Don't know how you remember it."

"The same way you remember how to plumb a bathroom, I suppose."

"Like you said, every man to his trade."

"What I said was, every man to his last. I took my metaphor from the cobblers."

"And it sounds like a load of old cobblers to me."

"Could be," I said.

"Only kidding," he said.

"Me too," I said.

"Fiorella writes poetry."

"Really?"

"I could show you some if you like. I've no idea if it's any good."

"Everybody has to start somewhere. You should see my stuff when I was her age. Embarrassing!" I said, and, checking the map again, added, "Take the second to the right and go straight on to the next lay-by."

Five
- - - - - - -

|

How we dote on gear.

The clothes, the gadgets, the tools of our chosen pleasures.

With many people, perhaps most, all this clobber appeals because of our obsession with fashionable regalia.

I sometimes wonder whether most people choose their hobbies because they lust after the gear more than for the benefits of the activities themselves.

Togged up for fishing, Karl didn't just look the part, he *was* the part. And he was so adept with his rod and line it was hard to imagine him ever being a learner. While he was fishing, he was a man at home with himself.

I noticed his fishing togs and his gear were well used, and

not only well used but old-fashioned. Perhaps he couldn't afford new stuff and had bought it all secondhand?

||

You want to know about love what I think about it but I don't know about it not like you mean. I Googled it and it said there are a lot of kinds of love and I think you only mean what people call true love which I don't think is such a good word because love can only be true because if its not its not love is it. anyway all I can tell you is I like being with you and think about you all the time— well not all the time, you cant think about anyone all the time can you because you have to think of other things like when I'm at work if I don't think about what I'm doing I can make mistakes which can be very serious like the other day when I was NOT thinking about what I was doing because I was thinking about you and I forgot to tighten up a clamp on a joint and there was a leak when we turned the water on again and there would have been a flood if I hadn't been there to turn it off and tighten up the clamp. what I mean is I do think about you a lot and want to be with you, I won't say all the time because no one wants to be with the same person all the time do they— be honest but I want to be with you more than

I want to be with any one else, you interest me more than any one else and make me laugh and say things I haven't thought like that before which are important points about love I think and also other important points are respect and admiration which both of which I have for you but what I think you want me to say is that I am in love with you which you say you are with me but this is what I don't know about, well not yet even if I think I am because I don't have anything to compare it with in my life, I mean I haven't been in love before so how do you know

III

Because the early spring day was too cold to sit for long, I read Karl's letter, then took a walk along the riverbank, content in that beautiful place, one of the best in England, to watch some mallards, gem-bright in their mating colours, and let my mind wander along its own track, remembering my wife, Jane, and thinking how much she would have loved it here, until the sun burnt off the overcast, and warmed the day with a foretaste of summer.

I kept well away from Karl so as not to disturb him or the fish. But by midday, having had breakfast so early and the crystal air and exercise giving me an appetite, my stomach was grumbling for lack of its mid-morning coffee and wanting its lunch earlier than usual.

I set up a couple of fold-up camp stools in the dapple of sun and shade between two trees in sight of Karl, who was up to his thighs in the river, laid out the picnic on a fallen tree trunk, and hoped Karl might notice and join me.

I'm sure he'd have gone on fishing all day without a break, lost in the rhythm of casting and dancing his barbed fly on the frobbling water as he wound it in, if he hadn't moved a few metres downstream and was so intent on the spot he was aiming to land his fly he hadn't noticed an overhanging tree, which was in the direct path of the flight of his line. When he whipped it behind him before casting it forward, the hooked fly snagged a branch, and Karl found he'd caught a tree instead of a fish.

As he waded out of the river to disentangle his line, he looked sheepishly around, and saw me watching, unable to keep a grin off my face. For a second he was torn between anger and embarrassed laughter, and, choosing laughter, he shrugged his shoulders, retrieved his fly, rewound his line and joined me.

Then without a word, he set to on the food. I'd made a mix of sandwiches: egg, bacon and tomato; ham, cheese and pickle; cucumber and avocado; chicken, onion and stuffing. He went through half a dozen before I'd finished two.

I learned that day the one-track-minded intensity of Karl's concentration. He didn't like doing more than one thing at a time. And once involved, he'd stick at it for hours.

I also learned, as I'll describe in a minute, the power of some emotions he kept locked away, because he knew that if he let them loose they'd undo his self-control.

"Good nosh," he said when he'd taken the edge off his appetite. "Thanks."

"You're welcome," I said. "Have as much as you want. By the way, I've read your letter."

"Pretty bad, isn't it?" he said, biting into a ham-and-cheese sandwich. "Rammed it down and didn't read it afterwards."

"It's not that bad. I like its honesty. Just needs a bit of tidying up. Shall I do it for you?"

"Please."

"One point, as you mention points."

"What?"

"Do you think you're in love with Fiorella or not?"

"Like I said, I don't know."

"But would you say you've felt stronger and stronger about her since you first met?"

He stopped chewing and thought a moment.

"Yes, I have," he said, took an egg sandwich and started eating again.

"So you could honestly say you love her, and love her more and more?"

He nodded. "I suppose so, yes."

"Maybe you should tell her that? It would help her understand what you feel about her, and it seems to me that's really what she wants to know."

More thinking without chewing.

"That would be OK, yes."

"Would it help if I added a couple of sentences saying that?"

"OK."

He finished off the sandwiches and drank a can of Coke.

I knew him well enough already to sense when he'd had enough of a topic that cut too close to the bone.

I asked, to change the subject, "Caught much?"

"Not too bad. Five."

"Taking them home to eat?"

"See what there is at the end of the day. Pick a couple of the best and put the rest back."

"They're in a keep net?"

"Would you like some?"

"One would be nice, thanks. Very fond of trout."

"How d'you do it?"

"Filleted. White wine. Seasoning. Twenty minutes in the oven."

"Never done it like that."

"Very easy. Very tasty."

"I'll give it a go."

"You certainly have plenty of gear."

He nodded and launched into a mini lecture, showing me each piece as he talked about it. He was, he told me, a Hardy fan—which meant nothing to me. An old firm, I gathered, much admired for their quality. His rod was a Hardy Demon, thirteen foot long, three sections that pulled apart. He described what he liked about it and one or two features he didn't like. His reel was a Cascapedia. (I thought he'd meant Cassiopeia, but on repeating it, as you do when someone uses a word new to you, like a child learning to speak, I was firmly corrected, the syllables of the word clearly enunciated—Cas-ca-pe-di-a.) Its characteristics were itemised and demonstrated. I asked about the flies he used. He opened a little metal box full of them, each fly resting in its own compartment on a bed of cotton wool. They were beautiful little works of representational art, each one different in shape and colours. They had names as alluring as their appearance. I remember March Brown, Morning Glory, Wickham's Fancy, Red Tag and Pheasant Tail. Karl talked about when he'd use them, in which conditions. He handled them with the delicacy of a lepidopterist holding a live and fragile butterfly.

What struck me most as he talked was how fluent he was. Not a hint of hesitation, no stumbling over words or thoughts, his explanations clear and the information well ordered. Just as when fishing he was so absorbed in what he was saying, and in showing me the gear was so full of quiet unselfconscious enthusiasm, that he infected me with his fascination and pleasure. This was a mature and confident Karl, different from the uneasy and sometimes awkward boy who balked at saying anything about himself, who tripped and stumbled when he did, and who couldn't write a reasonably competent sentence.

I watched and listened with admiration. Had Fiorella

seen him like this? If she had, it was obvious why she wanted him, despite his hang-ups and his difference from herself.

Finally he paused and, re-collecting himself, gave me a smile, shrugged and said, "Sorry. Didn't mean to go on like that."

"Not a bit. I enjoyed it," I said. "I can see you like your fishing."

"I do," he said.

"What's the best thing about it?"

He replied without a second's thought, "I forget myself."

"You mean, all your worries, that sort of thing?"

"No. I mean me. Myself."

"Why do you like forgetting yourself?"

"Dunno. Just do."

His shifty look gave him away. He knew all right, but didn't want to explain.

Time to change the subject again.

I thought a moment before saying, "Fiorella wants to know what you believe. Quite a few of her questions are on that topic, aren't they?"

"Yes. But I don't know."

"Well, for a start, do you believe in God? Any god?"

"No."

"What, then? I'm sure you've thought about it."

"I have. And if I hadn't, Fiorella would have made me."

"Does she believe in God?"

"Yes."

"She's Christian and goes to church?"

"No."

"What then?"

"She says she's working it out for herself."

"And wants you to do it with her?"

"Yes."

"So what did you tell her?"

He looked towards the river, wanting, I think, to get back to his fishing, and said with strained tolerance, "What is, is."

"What is, is?"

"What is, is."

"Meaning?"

He glanced at me warily. He really wasn't comfortable with this kind of talk.

"What is there, is there. The river is there. The trees are there. You are there."

I thought for a moment.

I said, "You remind me of a saying by an old Chinese or Japanese philosopher, I forget which. He said, 'When I was young, I thought a river was a river and a mountain was a mountain. When I grew up, I thought a river wasn't a river and a mountain wasn't a mountain. Now I am old, I think a river is a river and a mountain is a mountain.'"

Karl laughed. "I like that. I wish I'd said it."

Laughing too, I said, "You will, Karl, you will."

He laughed again, and took another sandwich and started eating hungrily again.

I was beginning to know him. That movement meant *Enough of this.*

"Well, anyway," I said, "I'm no expert, but it seems to me you're a pretty good fisherman."

"Except when I'm catching trees instead of fish."

Again we laughed.

"How did you get to be so good?" I said. "Did you teach yourself?"

He looked away.

"No . . . My dad."

There was a sudden brittle silence.

Why? Something to do with his father, obviously, but what?

Everything about him at that moment warned me not to ask.

I got out the flask of coffee. Asked him if he'd like some. He said nothing. Head still turned away. No movement.

I filled two mugs and held one out to him.

He took it without looking at me and drank.

Nothing more was said.

When he'd finished his coffee, he stood up and gathered his gear, still avoiding me.

"Thanks," he said and paused on the brink of saying something more, but all that came out was, "See you later."

And he strode off to the river.

A raw nerve touched and no recovery.

IV

Dear Fiorella [or whatever],

You asked me to tell you about love and what I think about it. The trouble is, I don't know quite what I think about it, because I don't know a lot about it. Or at least not like I think you mean.

Don't laugh, but I Googled it. There're pages about it. A lot about different kinds of love. I won't bore you by reporting on all of it.

I think what you mean and want me to tell you about is what people call true love. I don't actually think "true love" is such a good term because love can only be true. If it isn't true it can't be love.

Am I in "true love" with you? All I can tell you is I want to be with you more than I want to be with anyone else. You interest me more than anyone else. You make me laugh and you say things I haven't thought before. These are important points about love, I think, don't you?

Other important points are respect and admiration. I respect and admire you.

But what I think you want me to say more than anything is that I am in love with you, which you say you are with me. But I have to be honest and say I don't know. Well, not yet, even if I think I am, which I do. What makes it difficult for me is that I don't have any previous experience to go on. I have nothing to compare what I feel for you with what I've felt for anyone.

I know some people talk about love at first sight. But I've heard other people say they fell in love gradually. I can tell you that my feelings for you have grown stronger the more I've got to know you. And I want to go on getting to know you more and more. I would call what I feel for you love.

This is the best I can say at present.

With love [?], Karl

V

For the next hour or so I rewrote Karl's letter, and took another stroll along the river.

When I got back, Karl was sitting on the bank, his rod by his side, hunched over, his head in his hands.

For a moment I thought he was resting. But no. Instinctively, I felt he was brooding on whatever had upset him earlier.

I debated whether to leave him alone or to make sure he was all right and sit with him for a while. I decided it was better to make sure he was all right, even if it proved a wrong move.

Karl didn't stir when I sat down beside him.

We were silent for some minutes before he raised his

head and clasped his hands in front of him, his elbows resting on his knees.

A few more minutes went by in silence.

Then he took a deep breath, let it out.

"My dad died when I was twelve."

He didn't wait for me to say anything.

"I know it's a long time ago," he went on. "You'd think I'd be over it by now."

I heard him swallow hard.

"I lied to you," he continued when he had gained control again. "I have been here before. Quite a few times . . . It was my dad's favourite place . . ."

Another stumble. Another swallow before he could go on.

"I wanted to prove to myself it was OK, I'd be able to fish here again . . . Remember him . . . Us fishing together."

This time he stopped because he wanted to, not because of a surge of emotion.

"I was all right this morning. It was good. I felt he was with me. Like he always was, standing beside me, telling me where to cast and how to do it better . . . But when you asked about learning . . ."

A long silence.

A flash of shining blue along the river in front of us.

Karl pointed.

"See it?"

"Yes."

"Kingfisher."

"Oh yes! I've never seen one before. Beautiful."

He smiled his pleasure.

I said, "Why come back today especially?"

The smile vanished but he kept my eyes, and with self-defensive sharpness said, "Because today is the sixth anniversary."

"I see. So it's a commemoration as well as a challenge?"

He nodded and turned away.

I needed to move. Sciatica and old man's bones didn't like squatting on the damp, cold ground for long. But something else. Something worse. Jane.

I stood up.

"Maybe you should do something."

"What d'you mean?"

I could tell from the way he said it that he knew what I was getting at.

It seems to me there are two kinds of people. There are those who prefer everything to be spelt out, clear and direct, nothing left to doubt. The others are people who prefer to read between the lines, who don't want every *i* to be dotted, every *t* to be crossed. They need room to decide for themselves what you mean.

I have to confess that by nature I belong to the spellers-out. But I was learning that Karl belonged to the understaters, the ambiguists.

Sometimes the spellers-out need to restrain themselves, and sometimes the understaters need to be given a hint, a clue to help them.

I said, "Maybe you should do something to mark the day."

Karl stood up. We faced the river, side by side.

"Like what?" he said.

"I don't know. Something that would mean something to you. Something that would have meant something to your father."

He thought for a moment before saying with that defensive sharpness of tone again, "You mean something that will help me say good-bye?"

I didn't reply.

"That's what my mother keeps telling me. Let him go, she says."

"Maybe she's right."

"She's always right. That's the trouble."

"And you'd rather she wasn't."

He chuckled. "No." Looked serious again and said, "But I don't want to say good-bye. My dad was the best person in my life."

And he walked away.

Just as well. We were getting into deep water for him and for me, and I knew I'd be out of my depth.

Also I needed to visit a convenient clump of bushes.

VI

When I came back, I said, "Had enough? Ready for home?"

"You said about doing something."

52

"Yes?"

"Dad always did something. When he'd finished for the day. He always did the same thing."

"Yes?"

"He'd find a bit of stick. He'd cut notches on it, one for each of the fish he'd caught. Then he'd pack up to go. And the last thing he'd do was stand on the bank, say some words, always the same words, then throw the stick into the river."

"He did that every time?"

"Every time."

"A kind of ritual. Did you ask him about it?"

"My dad didn't talk much."

"Like father, like son," I said, smiling.

Karl returned the smile. "I'm a chatterbox compared to him."

"So you never asked?"

"I did once."

"What did he say?"

"'Never take anything for granted.'"

"'Never take anything for granted'? That was all?"

"Yes."

I thought for a bit.

"When I asked you what you believed, you said, 'What is, is.' Did you get that from your dad?"

He nodded and said, "I've found a stick."

He showed me an ash twig about an inch thick and a foot long.

"I've caught five today. I'll make five notches. Then I'll do what Dad did. Want to do it with me?"

We went to the edge of the bank.

Karl sat and cut five snicks through the thin bark, till the white of the wood showed through.

Then he stood up facing the river, me beside him.

He held the stick out in front of him, and in a voice only just loud enough to hear, intoned,

"Water brought thee.
Water take thee.
I have caught thee.
I shall eat thee.
Dwell in me,
As I in thee.
I give thanks
For water,
And for thee."

He dropped the stick into the river.
We watched it swirl away.

SIX

- - - - - - -

FOR TWO WEEKS AFTER THE FISHING TRIP I HEARD NOTHING from Karl.

Had I upset him? Was he sorry he'd told me about his father? Did he wish he hadn't shared the ritual at the end?

Every day I checked my emails, hoping to see his name, and kept my mobile phone beside me in case he sent a text.

I was surprised at myself. Yet not surprised. I knew he was helping me as much as I hoped I could help him, though he didn't know how, and I still wasn't certain myself.

In the few days after our trip I boned up on dyslexia, wanting to learn more than the sketchy general knowledge I already had.

I can't think without making notes, so I listed what I found out:

—*Dyslexia takes many forms.*

—*There's no one condition you can call dyslexia.*

—*There isn't even agreement on what the word means, except that it comes from an old Greek word meaning "difficulty with words and language."*

—*People with dyslexia usually have trouble with spelling, sometimes reverse numbers and letters—confusing* d *and* b, *for example—and have difficulty with cursive (joined up) writing.*

—*They have difficulty putting their thoughts down on paper—writing is often torture to them.*

—*They are often slow readers, and often need to read the same passage two or three times before they can understand it.*

—*They often mix up left and right, sometimes have difficulty finding their way around, even in familiar surroundings.*

—*They sometimes have difficulty finding the correct word, so they say "whatyoucallit" and "thingies," and get ordinary words twisted.*

—*Their vocabulary is often limited. They don't know as many words as they should. They suffer from verbal poverty.*

—*Because they have had difficulty with reading and writing, they feel they are failures, suffer from low self-esteem and embarrassment, and think they must be stupid. This is often reinforced by the way people treat them, especially if teachers do not understand their condition. Therefore they lack self-confidence.*

It was obvious that Karl suffered from some of these symptoms. Even though he'd only shown me printouts of his writing, when he must have used the spell-checker, I could tell he'd struggled when composing sentences and ordering his thoughts.

But when he talked about something that really interested him, like fishing or plumbing, he was fluent and mature and entirely coherent. You'd never have known he had trouble with words. His vocabulary was far from limited. I knew from his driving that he had no trouble with left and right or finding his way. As a plumber his hand-eye coordination must be good, as I knew it was from watching him fish. Yes, he didn't like talking about his feelings, but many people don't who are not dyslexic.

There was a plethora of guff on the internet about dyslexia, thousands of references. But as usual, finding clear and brief answers to straightforward and simple questions wasn't so easy.

What was certain, which I had already thought for myself but which the experts confirmed, was how best you can help someone who is dyslexic.

They all mentioned the frustration sufferers feel when they are clever, as Karl certainly was, but can't be clever in reading and writing.

Their difficulties are caused by a difference in their brain and the way it works, not because they are lazy or stupid.

They need to be sure you won't make fun of their difficulties, or do anything that makes them look silly in front of others.

Most of all, you need to give them confidence, and to

know, really *know*, that they aren't odd or stupid or have a weird illness.

What they have is different from most people, but is not a disability. In fact, because of their difficulty with language their brains open up new pathways that the brains of the rest of us don't. And those pathways often enable them to be more creative than people who aren't dyslexic.

I was sympathetic with Karl because I'd had trouble with reading and writing when I was a kid. Bad spelling, a slow reader. In fact, couldn't read at all till I was eight. In those days, ordinary people, including teachers, had never heard of dyslexia. So teachers especially thought you were "dull," "not very clever," "thick." "He's a little slow" was how a teacher expressed it to my worried mother. She meant I was halfway to being the village idiot. Not so, as it turned out. I don't blame her. She didn't know better. But that didn't prevent me feeling I was a dead loss, a failure at the two things everybody knows are the most important in our word-dominated society: being able to read and write well.

But something bothered me. Yes, it was true that he showed some of the signs of dyslexia, but not to a serious extreme. And, yes, he was finding ways of dealing with the difficulties—his brain must be opening up the new pathways. And, yes, the last thing you'd say about him was that he was slow-witted. Quite the opposite. He was clever, thoughtful and creative. But I sensed it wasn't only dyslexia that troubled him. It wasn't dyslexia that was jamming up his feelings about himself. And it wasn't dyslexia that prevented him talking about himself. As a recovered dyslexic, I know that I've never been shy of talking about myself and my deepest feelings—so long as it was to someone I liked and trusted.

Of course, he might not want to talk about himself because he was happier keeping himself to himself.

But that's not what I sensed with Karl. I became convinced he was bottling up a brew of strong feelings that he wanted to let out but couldn't. There'd been three or four times when I felt he might explode. And one moment when he had. The moment by the river when he talked about the death of his father. Then I'd caught a glimpse of his inner self. And he was no longer an eighteen-year-old young man, expert at fishing, competent as a plumber, no doubt tough on the rugby field, and good at chess—the young man Fiorella had no doubt fallen for. But instead, he was a little boy, a distressed twelve-year-old, vulnerable, hurt, and grieving.

Hang on, though, I told myself. You could be wrong. It's always a mistake to think you know what makes someone tick.

Karl was right. Actions speak louder than words. When all is said and done, you can only go by what people do, not by what they say.

Now, two weeks after the revelation of his father's death, I'd heard nothing from him. This action, this silence, meant more than words.

But then, just when I'd decided he wanted nothing more to do with me, his name popped up on my screen.

His email's subject line said:

Fiorellas poem

His message read:

Fiorella sent me this poem, is it any good, don't know much about poems, hope you ok, meet tuesday 8?

Not shut out after all!

One of my weaknesses is always to fear the worst. And another is to think that anything that goes wrong is my fault.

I replied:

Tuesday. 8:00 p.m. Meal at the pub? My treat.

He replied pronto:

ok but on me

Here's the poem:

Two poems for Karl

1	2
Do you believe—	I would be known
As I believe—	As known as
What there is	Knowing can be
Is all there is?	By you
	Who knows
Do you believe—	How knowing is
As I believe—	That knows
That we are	No knowing.
More than we	
Yet know?	And I would know
	As known as
Do you believe—	Knowing can be
As I believe—	The you
You are	Who keeps me
Who I would know	From knowing
And I am	The you
Who you would know	Who knows
So you can be	No knowing.
What you are	
And I can be	
What I am?	

seven

"IS IT ANY GOOD?" KARL ASKED WHEN WE WERE SETTLED TO steak and chips (him), sausage and mash (me), a pint of Brothwaite's Best Brew (him), a glass of red wine (me).

"It's clever."

"Does 'clever' mean good with poems?"

"Not necessarily."

"So what does?"

"Why ask me?"

"You're the expert."

"Me?"

"You're a writer."

"I write stories, not poems."

"So? It's all words, isn't it?"

"Does being an expert plumber make you an expert gastroenterologist?"

"A what?"

"Gastroenterologist. An expert on your guts."

"What's that got to do with it?"

"They're both experts with pipes."

"D'you have to talk about that when we're eating?"

"You're finicky, then?"

"Only on Tuesdays. So you don't know if Fiorella's poem is any good?"

"Good is a dodgy word when it comes to poetry. To anything actually."

"You're as bad as a politician. Can't you give a straight answer to a simple question?"

"The trouble is it's not a simple question. Nothing is when it comes to poetry. But to satisfy your hunger for my inexpert opinion, I'll admit that her poem may be too clever for its own good."

"You mean she's up her bum?"

"I thought you didn't like that sort of talk on Tuesdays?"

"But is she?"

"I wouldn't put it that way. What I mean is, Fiorella is clearly a clever girl, clever with words. And like a lot of clever people, when they try to write poetry, they think it has to be clever-clever to prove how clever they are. And because they tend to read clever-clever poets they copy them. Well, sometimes they pull it off and sometimes they don't."

"And you think Fiorella hasn't?"

"She has and she hasn't."

"There you go again! Look, if somebody asks me whether a bit of plumbing is any good, I can tell them how well the pipes are fitted and how good the joints are and that sort of stuff. You're a writer. Why can't you tell me how well Fiorella has done her poetry plumbing?"

"All right."

I pushed away my plate of half-eaten sausage and mash, took a printout of Fiorella's poem from my pocket and laid it on the table between us.

"This repetition," I said, "'Do you believe as I believe.' That's all very neat, and she's making a nice point of connecting what you believe, which she must have got from you, and you telling her about yourself. Or rather, not telling her about yourself, which is implied not said."

"And that's good?"

"It's not bad. If she'd left it at that, you could give her, let's say, six out of ten."

"Now you're sounding like a teacher as well as a politician."

"The second part of the poem, the stuff about know and knowing, now that's over the top, in my inexpert opinion."

"Like, you mean if it was plumbing there'd be too many unnecessary pipes and joints?"

"Something like that. Listen, I'll read it to you. That's the best test of poetry: How does it sound?"

"Like does the water run smoothly through the pipes?"

"Exactly."

I read the second part of the poem aloud.

"Oooo! Get her!" hooted a shaven-headed, beer-gutted character of the hot metal variety sitting at the next table. "Poncing with the pooerterwy!"

What followed took my breath away.

Karl turned his head to the intruder, gave him what my mother used to call "a look that could kill," and in a voice of quiet and controlled violence said, "This is the polite version: Mind your own frigging business."

Pause. Tense silence.

Nothing was forthcoming from our gutsy neighbour. He tried to return Karl's uncompromising glare but wasn't up to the confrontation.

His pals sniggered.

Karl waited a further freezing moment before turning back to me, gave me a smile as fresh as spring, and said, "I see what you mean. It's a bit like chewing string."

And he went into an exaggerated riff, over-pronouncing with a po-faced expression and in a voice that mimicked a pompous preacher, the words "Known knowing who knowing knows no knowing who knows you knowing but who knows knowing no knowing but knowing knows knowing when knowing is known . . ."

The effect of which, after the drama of the belligerent neighbour, reduced me to overcompensating laughter, and Karl too when he stopped his blether.

But this was not the end of it. Unfortunately, I was not witness to the debacle.

When we'd run out of laughter and generally calmed down, I said, "Really, we're mean, taking the mickey out of Fiorella's poem. We ought to be ashamed."

"Why?" Karl said. "She's not here. What she doesn't *know*—" Repeating that word almost undid us again, but I held up a warning finger and swallowed the rising chortle.

"Well," Karl continued, also suppressing the urge, "it can't hurt her, can it? And, anyway, even if she was here, it'd be a pretty bad job if she couldn't laugh at herself. I wouldn't want a girlfriend who can't laugh at herself."

"There is that," I said. "Take your work seriously, but don't take yourself too seriously, you mean?"

"Something like that."

"But the thing is," I went on, "what Fiorella doesn't understand is that some people aren't word people like she is."

"What are they, then?"

"They do things. They have to do something before they can say what they mean."

"And you're saying I'm like that?"

"Aren't you?"

Reluctantly: "Maybe."

"Anyway," I said, taking the hint not to pursue the idea. "Fiorella wants a reply, doesn't she? She wants to know what you think. You can hardly tell her you think she's disappearing up her own fundament, now can you?"

"No. But what can I say? I mean, that's honest and not bullshit?"

"Putting myself in her shoes—"

"I'm not sure I want to picture that."

"What helps me as a writer when I ask someone to tell

me what they thought of something I've just written—when it's still raw, I mean, and so am I—is that they tell me which bits they liked. That's encouraging, and gives me confidence. And we all need encouragement. As you," I added, looking him seriously in the eyes, "ought to know." His face blanked. He nodded and looked at the table.

I pushed the printout in front of Karl, stood up and said, "While I visit the wailing wall, take another gander at Fiorella's poem, and see if there's anything you can say you genuinely like. A word, a phrase, a line, a stanza. Anything will do. Then we'll compose a suitable critique."

And I went off to the men's.

While I was there, I heard a sudden rowdy noise followed by a thud like a sack of potatoes hitting the floor. But I was enjoying so much the pleasure of relief—a slow process for men of my age who are suffering the symptoms of trouble with the "waterworks"—and was thinking at the same time about what Karl might write to Fiorella, that I paid only quarter ear attention to the bangarang going on outside.

But when I'd washed my hands, checked myself in the mirror and left the loo, Tom, the publican, who I knew well, was waiting for me in the passage. And he was not happy.

"That young guy who's with you."

His tone as well as his looks indicated trouble.

"Karl? What about him?"

"There's been a bit of a fracas."

"A fracas?"

"I'm not sure what happened, but from what I can gather, him and one of the fellers at the next table got across each other and your guy ended up flooring the other one."

"What? Karl? Never!"

"I didn't see it, so I don't know the ins and outs."

"I can't believe Karl is to blame, even if he did it. He's not the sort to pick a fight."

"I don't care who's to blame. I can't allow that sort of behaviour. Bad for business."

"Where is he now?"

"I turfed the lot of them out and told them not to come back. They're barred. Your lad's outside. The other one was carted off by his pals."

Gobsmacked is the pub word for how I felt. And a sense of guilt that in some way it was my fault.

"I'm sorry," I said. "I'd better—" And made a move to leave.

"The bill," the publican said.

In my confusion I thought he was referring to the police.

"Is that necessary?"

He had the grace to laugh. "The meal?"

What he meant seeped through.

"Oh! Yes, sorry. Look, I'll come back as soon as I've checked on Karl, OK?"

Tom nodded and shrugged.

"You're a good neighbour," he said. "No hard feelings. It's on the house."

I didn't even think to thank him.

It was dusk. Cold and damp.

Karl was sitting, hunched over one of the picnic tables on the pub terrace. No one else around. I sat down opposite him. But now the sparky, funny young man I'd eaten with had disappeared leaving behind a wary, morose, locked-up teenager almost literally shrunk into himself, who wouldn't or couldn't look me in the eye.

I waited for him to say something. But nothing.

The cold was already getting to me. I wasn't dressed for outside.

"Fancy a cup of coffee?" I said, hoping we might go home where we could at least be warm while Karl gloomed.

He shook his head.

Impasse.

"Look," I said as light-toned as I could manage when my patience weakened. "I don't know what happened. If you don't want to tell me, that's OK. But I would like to know if you're all right."

He nodded.

"You're not hurt?"

He shook his head.

Pause.

But the cold was slicing my bones.

"Well," I said, "if it's OK with you I'll say good night and push off home."

No response.

I stood up. Was about to leave when: "He said something I didn't like."

I waited for more. None was offered.

"What was it?" I asked.

"Doesn't matter."

"It mattered enough for you to have a go at him, if what the publican says is true."

"It was about us."

"Ah!"

"But I didn't do anything then. Only told him to shut it. But the others egged him on."

"So?"

"He stood up and when I wouldn't, he said something worse than before."

"And this time?"

Really, with Karl in this mood it was like extracting teeth with a pair of tweezers.

"I stood up."

"And what then? All of this must have happened pretty quickly. I wasn't in the loo *that* long."

"It did."

"So what happened?"

"He said something else. Punched me in the chest. I gave him a chop and he went down."

"A *chop?* What kind of a chop?"

70

"Instinctive."

"Where did you hit him?"

"The throat. Side of my hand."

"And that knocked him out?"

"Not exactly."

"What, then?"

"He started choking."

I couldn't help smiling.

"But he's all right?"

"He'll live."

"Let's hope so. And let's hope he doesn't bring charges."

"He won't."

"How can you be so sure?"

"Pride."

"Meaning?"

"Last thing he wants is for it to get round that some little poofter dropped him."

"That's what he called you?"

He nodded.

"And me?"

"Yes."

"And that's what riled you?"

"No."

"What did, then?"

"Nasty-minded bigot."

I took a deep breath and paused for thought.

We'd both had enough for that night. We both needed to

recover. It was only now, when I knew what had happened, that my mind caught up with my feelings and needed time to sort them out and get back into balance. I guessed the same was true for Karl. And both of us would do best on our own. But how to part without hurting his feelings or appearing to desert him when he was clearly in bad shape?

It was Karl who decided, thank goodness.

"I'd better be off," he said. "I'm sorry. I messed up."

I wanted to let him know I didn't mind. "Sure you wouldn't like a coffee and talk a bit more?"

"Thanks, but I've caused enough trouble for one night."

"You didn't cause the trouble. He did."

"No. Well."

"We still have to decide what you'll say about Fiorella's poem."

"I'll be in touch. OK?"

"OK. Good night, then."

"See you," he said and fetched his bike.

As I watched him pedal away, I wondered what it was like to be Karl Williamson. What was it like to live inside his head? What did he think and feel, awake and asleep? Who was he? Did he know himself? If he did, he certainly wasn't letting on. Tonight I'd seen two Karls, almost extremes of each other, like two hemispheres of himself.

But then, I said to myself, don't I have within me more than one self? I've seen two Karls tonight, but I've been two of myself as well. We've both been our summer selves, bright and confident and warm, and our winter selves, distressed and dark and cold.

And anyway, who knows all of me? No one. How can anyone know me, when I've spent more than seventy years trying to work out who I am and still don't know all of the answer. Why should Karl know who he was when he'd had much less time to work it out?

EIGHt

- - - - - - -

I HAD A BAD NIGHT AFTER THE INCIDENT IN THE PUB.

I was worried about Karl. We'd parted on an awkward note. How would he be feeling? I hadn't handled things well.

My impulse was to get in touch. But I'd made a rule from the beginning never to take the initiative but always to wait for Karl to make the next move.

The young are only interested in themselves, and least of all in old people. The old are there to help them. Once the young have what they want, they forget you. I don't blame them. I was just the same. We're made that way.

But sometimes you do have to take the initiative, you do have to make a move. There are times when the old do know better. I wondered whether this was such an occasion, but decided against it. If Karl needed me, he'd let me know.

Patience. The virtue we need most in old age.

But something else kept me awake. My prostate trouble. Maybe the upset in the pub and my worries afterwards made it worse. Tension, stress, does make many ailments worse, and causes some. Whether the upset caused it or not, that night it was so bad even the strongest analgesics I had in the house didn't dull the pain enough to let me sleep. Up till now it had been worse sometimes more than others, and sometimes it was hardly noticeable. But on the whole it was getting worse all the time.

There's nothing like pain for turning you in on yourself. By morning I wasn't thinking about Karl. My anxiety focused entirely on the prospect of an operation and my horror of hospitals. How much I hate those places! But pain not only turns you in on yourself, it reaches a point when you'd do anything to get rid of it. So I made an appointment to see the doctor. I'd been putting this off in the desperate hope that the trouble might cure itself. But reality kicked in, and I knew the sooner the condition was dealt with the better.

I mention this only because eventually it had repercussions with Karl.

Late that evening, when I was checking my emails for the last time before going to bed, Karl's name appeared on the screen with the following message:

I dictating this on voice recognition program called Dragon. They gave it to me when they were trying to help me at school with my dyslexia, I thought I'd use it now because it might help me to say what I want to say about fur ellas poem because I can do it better dictating than buy typing it though when I was trying to use this machine in the past. It made as many mistakes as when I do it typing. But I don't have to think about spelling or punctuation, if it gets them wrong that is fault not mine and also I forget most of the commands you have to use. I expect there will be even more mistakes but I'm not going to read this because if I do I probably wouldn't send it. So I'm sorry if there are a lot of mistakes

What I want to say to fur ella is I don't know much about poetry so I'm not the right person to ask about it. I do quite like her poem and I think I see what she's getting at which is just another way of saying she wants to know all the stuff about me that I can't tell her, it's just I don't really know what to say, I mean, if you ask me about fishing or rugby or chess. I would know what to say. I can only talk about things that I know about and things that I believe in, yes, please, I'll have a cup, damn, sorry it will have written that down. It was my mum asking if I want a cup of coffee and I forgot the Dragon writes down everything you say

As far as love is concerned there are all sorts of kinds and she wants me to say what I mean about. When it comes to her. I tried to tell her what I think in one of the letters we wrote earlier. I don't think this is getting very far is it. So maybe if you could just write something for me on the lines of. I like her poem, and I'm glad she wrote to me and I do think it's very clever and I hope she can write more and wish I could write a poem to her but I can't, like I explained to you in the pub

What I'd like to do is go somewhere, take a tent and camp out together where there is some decent fishing. We could take the travelling chess set and she could take her book and do her writing while I fish, I think we would get to know each other much better than we can when we only see each other once a week and then not always on our own in private and it's easier to talk I mean about myself in the country when I'm fishing as I think you found out. So maybe I can tell her then the stuff about myself she wants to know

Camping together and living together like that would be a kind of poetry to me living it instead of writing it I could certainly show her what I mean. That sounds like I mean sex. We do talk about sex, it will be no surprise to know we do it but not with plenty of time and private which isn't the best way but I'm not talking about sex I'm talking about living together properly on our own. Even though only for a short time but that would be enough for a start. With her half term holiday coming up I can take a week's holiday from work and I've got all we need, tent, sleeping bags, cooking gear

What do you think would it be a good idea to write something like that to her and if you do could you write it and send it to me so I can send it to her as before

I'm sorry about the business at the pub. I know it upset you. It has upset me to but it all happened so quick and I just acted by instinct and that guy really did ask for it but I'm sorry it happened I should have known better and just walked away but I do have a hot temper sometimes and he hit the spot Karl

This made me smile and raised my spirits. The best relief, if not cure, for most ailments. And because, when the prostate pain is on, it's worse in bed at night, and Karl's email had restored my energy, I was glad of the excuse to put off going to bed and spent an hour drafting what I'd come to think of as "a Fiorella letter" and sent it. In a covering note, I said:

Seems to me your own typing plus spell-check is a lot better than what Dragon does for you.

Yes, I was upset after the pub, but only because I knew you were. Not your fault. There have been times in my life I've walked away when, looking back, I think it would have been better to stand my ground. But at the time it's hard to know which is best or the right thing to do. I agree, letting the other guy call the shots when the shots are violent, even if you can't avoid it, leaves you feeling the loser. Whatever you do and whatever the outcome, you feel you've let yourself down.

Write it off to experience, which is the name, Oscar Wilde said, we give to our mistakes. Besides, the man who never made a mistake never made anything, as Napoleon is supposed to have said, and he ought to know, he made plenty.

How's the following for Fiorella, who I'm amused to see your Dragon calls fur ella.

Hi, Fiorella [or whatever],

I've read your poem and thought about it a lot. I don't know anything about poetry. I don't read much of it—well, none, to tell the truth—and

I don't know what is supposed to make a poem good. But I can see your poem is clever. I mean, the way you use language, like the way you play on the word "know" and "knowing." It also made me think. I can see your poem is really another way of telling me you want to know all about me, and that love is about knowing all about the person you love, and the person you love knowing all about you.

You're probably right. But it isn't easy for me. I'm not sure why. The trouble is, it's hard to write down the answers to what you want to know. And telling you is hard as well, but not as hard as writing. But I haven't told you because we are never alone together for long enough for me to be relaxed the way I need to be to talk about myself.

Also, it seems to me some people are word people, like you, and some are not, like me. People like me need to do something before we can tell you what we want to say. We are action people.

I've thought about this a lot because of your poem, so it has worked like you wanted after all, because I have a suggestion.

As I say above, we need to be together long enough on our own for me to get into the right mood to tell you what you want to know.

My suggestion is that we go away for the week of your half-term holiday to a nice spot I know in the country by a river. We could camp there. I could fish (which helps me to relax a lot). You could read and write (or I could teach you to fish!). You could read me your poetry and explain about it. We could play chess.

Have you camped before? (See, there are things *I* still don't know about *you*!) I like it and am pretty good at it. I've got all the gear—big tent, sleeping bags, etc. I like cooking, as you know. You won't have to do any of that, if you don't want to. I will be camp manager, chief cook and bottle washer.

Doing that would be poetry to me.

What do you think?

Karl must have gone to bed late as well, because next morning when I booted up, an email from him was waiting, received at 1:33 a.m.

good, thanks. have sent. lot of work next 2 weeks, overtime as well, wont see you for a bit, will let you know about camping, hope you ok, karl

NINE

- - - - - - -

ABOUT A WEEK LATER, AN EMAIL FROM KARL. FIORELLA HAD
agreed to go camping with him.

Followed by two months without a word.

As I expected, I thought. The camping holiday has
worked out as he hoped. Now he doesn't need my help
anymore.

For me those two months were an uneasy time. The
doctor sent me to a consultant. He arranged tests. The tests
proved the specialist's diagnosis. Prostate trouble, but no
cancer.

With my ready agreement, they prescribed a new drug,
still in the testing stage, which might clear up the problem
without surgery. Anything to avoid hospital.

It took three or four weeks for them to get the strength

of the drug right, and for me to get over the side effects (some of which I'd rather forget than describe), but after that there was noticeable improvement. I slept at night, didn't need to go to the loo so often.

But I didn't forget Karl, thought of him often, wondered what he was up to. Had he passed his driving test? How was he getting on with Fiorella?

Then one morning just before lunch, a phone call.
Karl's mother, Mrs. Williamson, asking if she could come and see me.
Of course I said yes, full of curiosity, and also a touch of apprehension. She had sounded edgy.

She arrived an hour later.
She refused anything to eat or drink. We sat down, facing each other exactly as Karl and I had been the first time he visited, Mrs. Williamson looking awkward and uncomfortable on the sofa, me in my chair, trying to look relaxed when I wasn't.

"How's Karl?" I asked to get the conversation going.
She gave me a wary, inquiring look that reminded me of her son. But he didn't take after his mother in appearance. She was small, slight, probably petite and pretty and blonde before middle age filled her out and her hair turned to brown, already flecked with grey. Karl was tall, solidly

built, dark haired. But they had the same eyes and as we talked I noticed a number of little mannerisms and tricks of speech they shared.

"It's about Karl I'd like to talk to you," she said.

"Is he all right?" I asked, as calmly as I could, for if he was, why would she want to talk to me about him?

"He's not well," she said with defensive hardness.

A twinge of panic in my guts bent me forward with genuine anxiety. "I'm sorry to hear that. What's the matter?"

"Before I tell you," she said, hard still, "could I ask you something first?"

"Of course."

"*Why*," she said with more aggressive emphasis than I think she intended, because she tried to tone it down by repeating the word with less force. "Why are you so interested in my son?"

I sat back and waited a moment while I took in the implication of her question before saying:

"Forgive me for answering your question with a question. I know how irritating that is. But what do you know about Karl and me?"

Now it was her turn to wait. Were we going to play that awkward game "you answer my question before I answer yours"?

But she said, "I know he came to you about writing to Fiorella. But I also know you went fishing together, and you let him drive your car. And I know something happened that upset him the last time he saw you."

"But you don't know exactly what happened?"

"He won't tell me."

Was it right, I wondered, to tell Karl's mother about something he didn't want to tell her himself? Besides, I'm secretive by nature. I don't like telling what I know about one friend to another, or to anyone else. And I don't like people telling other people what they know about me.

But Mrs. Williamson had said Karl was ill, and she was suspicious of our friendship. A worried mother defending her son. She deserved an answer.

With a reluctance I hoped she heard in my voice I said, "The last time Karl and I met we had a meal in the local pub. I went to the loo. While I was there, a loud-mouthed man at the next table said some offensive things to Karl. Karl tried not to get involved, but the man wouldn't leave off. He had a go at Karl. Karl instinctively defended himself and knocked the man down. The publican wasn't too pleased and threw them all out."

I let Mrs. Williamson take this in before adding, "Karl wasn't to blame. But he was very upset. He thought he'd behaved badly."

She shook her head as if trying to clear it of ugly thoughts.

I said, "I've not seen Karl since then. He emailed that he and Fiorella were going camping. I haven't heard from him again."

There was a long silence.

Mrs. Williamson didn't look at me.

I said, "But that doesn't answer your question, does it?"

Now she did look at me, firm eyed. "No."

I said, "You know I'm a writer and that Karl asked me for help because Fiorella has read my books and wrote me a fan letter and told Karl about me."

"Yes, I know that."

"What you probably don't know is that eighteen months before Karl came to see me my wife died."

Mrs. Williamson's face changed. The hardness vanished.

I said hurriedly, "Please don't say anything. Jane's death is the worst thing that's ever happened to me . . . I was devastated . . . Fell into a deep depression. Like being in a very deep dark pit. A living grave . . ."

I stopped. Thank goodness, Mrs. Williamson remained still and silent. One movement, one word would have breached the dam.

I hadn't spoken about this to anyone for months. Why to a stranger?

When I could, I said, "The worst time was the first anniversary. All I wanted was to die."

It was hard to talk. I blew my nose, looked anywhere but at Mrs. Williamson.

Then on again. I had to finish.

"After that, I decided I had to pull myself out of the pit. Had to accept . . . Well. Anyway . . . But the thing is, I couldn't write. I mean, a book. Writing is my life. When

Jane died, I was in the middle of a novel. But afterwards, it seemed pointless. I couldn't write a word without feeling sick."

I blew my nose again.

"Only two things have ever really mattered to me. Our life together and writing novels. And it looked like I'd lost both."

I stopped again.

I heard Mrs. Williamson move and breathe out as if she'd held her breath all the time I was talking.

A long silence again.

Mrs. Williamson must have sensed it was safe to say something now. "Could I get you anything? A drink of water?"

I shook my head. An interruption would wreck whatever it was she and I were coming to.

"You miss your wife?" Mrs. Williamson said.

"Of course. You miss your husband?"

"Of course. How do you miss her?"

"What do you mean?"

"I always felt John was in front of me. Leading me. Now he's gone, it's like I've been abandoned. I'm on my own. And to be honest I feel lost half the time."

"I see. Odd you should put it like that. I always felt we were side by side. I'm a bit of a pessimist. Always expect the worst. She made me feel the future was possible."

"And you feel you don't have one now?"

"None."

"I think I might feel the same if I didn't have Karl. Have you any children?"

I shook my head again, words stymied.

Silence. We both shifted in our seats.

"Then," Mrs. Williamson said, "my Karl came to see you."

"Yes."

I managed to look at her.

Her eyes were full up too.

"Who has become . . . what? Like a son?"

I couldn't help laughing. Which was, as always, a blessed relief.

Looking puzzled, Mrs. Williamson said, "What's funny?"

"I'm sorry," I said. "It isn't like that. Not that I'd mind. I'd be proud to have Karl as a son. We're alike in a lot of ways, and I've come to admire him. But I wouldn't be a good father."

"Why not?"

"Too hung up on my work. It wouldn't be fair."

"So is it that he makes you feel young again?"

Another laugh. "No. I've given up any hope of that. I know I write fiction, but I'm a realist, not a fantasist."

This time Mrs. Williamson laughed as well. There was the delicious feeling of someone warming to you and you to them.

I said, "I know what you were thinking when you arrived. But it isn't that either."

"No. I'm sorry."

"Don't be. It was natural. We're conditioned to be suspicious these days."

"That's true. So what was it, then?"

I shrugged and smiled.

"You don't know about writers."

"I suppose I don't. You're the first I've met."

"Well, I'm afraid I must tell you that we're all disgracefully ruthless."

"Ruthless?"

"And unscrupulous."

She gave me that wary look again. "With my son? You were ruthless and unscrupulous with Karl?"

"I'll explain."

"I think you should."

"Writers. We can be as nice as pie personally. And genuinely. But the fact is, everything we do, everything that happens to us, everyone we know, well, it's all grist for the mill. Everything is raw material for work. For what we write."

"You're telling me Karl is only raw material for you?"

"No, no! Karl is Karl. Young. A breath of fresh air. And in need of help. I'm old. Tired. In need of fresh air. And in need of help."

"What kind of help?"

"To get me writing again."

"And how could Karl do that?"

"Just by being Karl and asking me to help him. I tried to

put him off. But he was determined. And very quickly that first time, when he explained his difficulties . . ."

I stopped, trying to assess whether she would understand what I was going to tell her.

"Yes?" she said.

I said, "I saw myself in him. He's stronger than I was at his age, but at the same time, he's as vulnerable as I was. And something else. I'm also dyslexic. Not seriously. I didn't know until a few years ago. But when I was a child, and people didn't know about it, I suffered because of it."

Mrs. Williamson gave me a long assessing look, which ended with a smile.

"I think," she said, "I'm beginning to understand."

"That's a relief."

"Helping my son was helping something in yourself?"

"Repairing an injury."

"And helping him to write to Fiorella got you writing again."

"Exactly. And you know, the strange thing is, it's only as I tell you this that I realise it's true."

"And what are you writing?"

"Nothing."

"I'm sorry? If he got you writing again how can you be writing nothing?"

"Well . . . Let's see . . . How can I put this? . . . A book, a novel, for me, always starts very vaguely. Like a cloud in my imagination. It drifts into view for no reason I know of. It's shapeless. Impossible to get hold of. But it's there. I know it's there. Floating about. But I have no idea what it's made of. What it wants to *be*. What it *means*. And over the years I've learned that what I have to do is wait. Wait for the cloud to take shape, become solid, become something I get hold of. Then I can try to catch it in words on paper. And it's only when I'm doing that, when I'm writing the words on paper, that I find out what it *is*, what it *means*, what it's trying to say to me."

Mrs. Williamson thought for a while. "So there's a cloud in your imagination, but you haven't started writing the words yet?"

"Correct."

"And being with Karl made that happen?"

"Yes. And I'll always be grateful to him."

She thought again.

"Does he know?"

"We've never talked about it."

More thinking.

"I understand what you went through when your wife died. I've been through it too. My husband died when Karl was twelve."

"I know."

This surprised her. "You know?"

"Karl told me."

"He did?"

"Yes. The day we went fishing."

She took a deep breath and her eyes filled again.

"Why does that surprise you?"

"He never tells anybody," she said. "He hates talking about it. Even to me."

I waited.

"It explains a lot," Mrs. Williamson said.

"Explains what?"

"When he told you about his father's death, did you tell him about your wife's?"

"No."

"Why not?"

"Because in my experience, when I'm upset, and I tell someone, and they say, 'Oh, I've been through that too' and start telling me about it, I always feel worse. Seems to me when someone tells you about something that's really upsetting them, what they want is for you to listen to their troubles, not talk to them about your own."

"I don't know. I think it's good sometimes."

"Perhaps."

"And you never told him what he was doing for you?"

"No."

"Well, as I say, I think that explains a lot."

"A lot about what?"

"His illness."

I'd forgotten. Talking about myself, answering her question, I'd forgotten. Panic in the guts again.

"What's happened?"

"Fiorella," Mrs. Williamson said.

"What about her?"

"She broke it off."

"What! Why?"

"He won't say."

"Oh Lord! When?"

"While they were camping."

"But that's weeks ago."

"He came home sooner than expected. He looked dreadful. I asked him what was the matter. He said Fiorella had dumped him and burst into tears. I haven't seen him cry since his father died."

"But he wouldn't explain?"

"No. For a few days he was all right. Or seemed to be. Very low, of course, but going to work. I thought he'd get over it. But then he suddenly got worse. He was getting his bike out to go to work one morning and had a sudden panic attack. Shaking all over, struggling for breath, sweating, couldn't stand, couldn't even hold a glass of water. Since then he hasn't been to work. Mostly stays in his room. Won't talk. Eats very little. He's lost a lot of weight. I don't know what he does all day. Stares at the wall or sleeps as far as I can make out."

"The doctor?"

"Yes, of course. He couldn't get any more out of Karl than me. Depression, he says. Because of the breakup."

"So what has he done?"

"Prescribed antidepressants. Offered to arrange for Karl to see a psychotherapist, but Karl refuses. I can't get him to leave the house. Won't take any exercise. And for someone as active as him . . ."

"Have you talked to Fiorella?"

"No."

"Wouldn't that be a good idea?"

"I like Fiorella. But to tell the truth, I never thought it would last."

"Why not?"

"They're both very young, young for their years. They'd fallen head over heels, but it was more passion than good sense. I was never sure what she found so attractive in Karl. In most ways they were chalk and cheese. She's a clever girl. Beautiful and talented. I got on well with her. But her parents weren't happy about it. They are very well off. Professional people. Didn't think a plumber was good enough for her."

"How d'you know?"

"Karl told me. And Fiorella used to joke about it. I think she quite enjoyed going against their wishes. Probably the first time she had."

"So it's not just a lovers' tiff?"

"I don't think so."

"No hope of them getting together again?"

"I'm not sure it would be a good thing if they did."

"You must be worried sick."

"I am. I don't know what to do. I'm afraid of what might happen if he goes on like this much longer . . . I'm desperate, to be honest."

By now I was so upset I needed to collect myself, and I could see Mrs. Williamson was on the edge of caving in as well.

Time for that panacea to which the English resort in times of crisis.

"Look," I said as levelly as I could. "How about a cup of tea while we take stock?"

She looked at me with a faint smile and said, "I'd like that. Thanks."

Ten minutes later we were sitting at the kitchen table exactly as Karl and I had sat that first time, had even talked while I made the tea about cooking and housekeeping, as he and I had. The relief of distraction. The comfort of familiar everyday chores. The consolation of food.

Then a silence that meant we were strong enough to face distress again.

I said, "When you asked to see me, you thought I might be in some way responsible for what's happened?"

"Yes."

"Do you still think so?"

"Not the way I did."

"But in some way?"

"I don't know. I don't know what to think now. All I'm sure of is that you helped Karl with Fiorella. Then she broke it off. And that made Karl ill."

She took a deep breath and let it out in a long sigh.

I said, "I'll do whatever I can. But I don't know what to suggest. Do you?"

She finished her tea. I offered more. She shook her head, and said, "One thing I've found out today is that

Karl talked to you about something he never ever talks to anyone else about. And for the few weeks when he and Fiorella were getting on well, he was the happiest since his father died. Now he's lost Fiorella and isn't seeing you, and he's worse than when his father died."

Easy to see what she was coming to.

"Do you think you could talk to him? He might open up to you."

My turn to take a deep breath.

"I'm not sure he would."

"I think he would. He talked a lot about how you made him think about things he hadn't thought about before. What he called your cool sense of humour. He took to you."

"Well, if you think it'll do any good, I'll try. But how?"

"You say you suffered from depression after your wife died?"

"Melancholia. Yes."

"So you understand how Karl is feeling."

"I do. But won't he think it odd if I suddenly contacted him after all this time?"

"You invent stories. Surely you can think of a convincing reason?"

"Is he writing emails?"

"I don't know. I don't think so. As I say, he doesn't seem to do anything."

"I can't just turn up. He'd be suspicious, wouldn't he?"

"Yes, he would. But there's something else."

"What?"

"I have to go to work every day. His father had his own small business. He was an electrical engineer. I did the office work and the accounts. After John died, I got something from a life insurance. I have the house, which we owned outright. John was determined about that in case the business failed. But there was nothing more. So I have to earn a living. And with Karl not working . . ."

"What do you do?"

"Secretary at our local primary school. I took the job because the hours were the same as Karl's. I could be at home when he was. He needed a lot of attention. I'm worried about leaving him on his own all day."

"Are you asking if I can be with him?"

"Not every day. Not all the time, of course. But maybe you could persuade him to go fishing? Or anything that would get him out of the house and give him something to do and think about besides whatever is going on in his mind at the moment."

I was stumped to know what to say. So much emotion, so many thoughts, all at once.

"I know it's a lot to ask," Mrs. Williamson said. "But if you could."

We sat in silence.

Finally, "I'm not saying I won't," I said. "I will. I'll do all I can. But I've never been quick. I'm a tortoise, not a hare. That's why I've written so few books. I need time to work things out."

Mrs. Williamson stood up. "I'm sorry. I understand."

I got up. "Let me brood about it overnight. I'll get in touch tomorrow. How shall I do that? Shall I phone you?"

"On my mobile, please. Karl doesn't answer the phone these days, but he does ask who's called. I think he always hopes it will be Fiorella."

She gave me her number.

I saw her out.

I went back into the kitchen to clear away the tea things, but before I could do it my knees gave way and I slumped into a chair feeling utterly exhausted, and burst into tears.

Ten

- - - - - - -

ANOTHER BAD NIGHT. THIS TIME THE KIND I HAVE IN THE MIDDLE of writing a novel, when I'm stuck. Thinking this way and that. What happens if . . . ? Supposing that . . . ? And no convincing answers.

What to do about Karl?

How to make contact without his suspecting contrivance and collusion with his mother?

What reason for contacting him? Not Fiorella, which would make matters worse.

Fishing? Perhaps, but why? He knew I wasn't a fisherman.

Such questions tangled in my mind till around five, when I fell asleep. And woke with a jangling start at nine thirty when the postman rang the front door bell. I stumbled downstairs, bleary and dazed. A book I'd ordered online.

No point in going back to bed. A shower revived me.

Breakfast calmed me. And as so often happens, a thirty-minute walk after breakfast clarified my jumbled nighttime thoughts and supplied the missing link.

What had happened during their time together that caused Fiorella to break up with Karl and go home on her own earlier than planned?

Whatever had happened was the cause of Karl's plunge into depression.

But Karl wouldn't tell his mother or the doctor. So why would he tell me?

If I knew what had happened and could think of a way to get in touch without scaring him off, he might open up as he had with me before, and I'd be prepared for what he told me. It's always easier to help someone when you know what is bothering them and have had time to think about it before getting involved.

So knowing what had happened was the key to unlocking Karl's locked-up soul.

The only other person who knew what had happened was Fiorella.

Maybe she would tell.

It was worth a try.

Hi, Fiorella.

I expect you remember our exchange of emails a year or so ago.

Forgive me for writing to you out of the blue,

but there's something important I'd like to ask you. Would you mind? Email, MSN, phone, as you prefer.

Luckily, it was a weekend. Fiorella was at home. She replied by MSN.

Hi. Is it about Karl?

Yes. How did you know?

Is it about when we went away together?

Yes.

Why do you want to know?

Karl is having a very bad time, which started after your trip. He won't say what happened. Only that you broke up with him.

But why do you want to know?

His mother thinks I might be able to help him, because I helped him before.

I know how you helped him and I was furious with you. And still am a bit.

Why?

Because I believed he wrote those emails but he didn't, you did. You shouldn't have done it. They were private.

He told you, did he, that I only wrote what he told me to write?

Yes. But writing is not just what is said, is it? It is how it is said. He didn't dictate the words to you, did he? They were your words not his. So I wasn't really getting him, was I?

Did Karl explain why he asked me to help?

Yes.

What did he tell you?

That he is dyslexic and was afraid I wouldn't go on with him if I saw his writing.

Did that matter to you?

No. Why should it? If he had told me from the start I would have helped him. Then he would not have needed to ask you.

So you broke it off with him because he involved me without telling you and you felt you couldn't trust him anymore?

No. That was not the reason. I was cross with him and with you and very upset at first. But I understood when he explained. And I would have forgiven him.

So why did you break up?

I don't want to tell you that. It has nothing to do with you.

I respect that, if it is what you decide. I'm sorry that I upset you. I did think it was risky. But Karl was so insistent and so desperate to do what you wanted him to do that I couldn't say no.

Well, alright. But that has nothing to do with breaking up with him.

Karl is very ill. If you still feel anything for him, you'll want to help him get better. His mother has asked me to try and help. But if I'm going to, I need to know what happened, and only you know that, apart from Karl, who won't say.

You are being very hard.

It's hard for me too. I feel I am partly to blame.

Let me think about it.

An hour or so later:

OK. But I want to do it properly. I'll send you an attachment later today.

ELeven

- - - - - - -

Fiorella's Attachment

I'm not sure I want to tell you this. I think I might regret it. I've told my parents what happened, well, almost all that happened, not all, but no one else. I'm only telling you because you emotionally blackmailed me. Do I still have feelings for Karl? Of course I do! And I don't want him to suffer because of anything I've done. Also because you were my favourite author. You are not now because of the emails, which, whatever you say, *were not his*. I still like your books but I don't like you.

Anyway, this is what happened.

Karl asked me to go away with him for the week of half-term holiday so that we could get to know each other better. He quoted some teacher or other who told him that the best way to find out if you really loved someone and could live with her was to go away with her to a remote cottage in bad weather, and if after a few days you didn't mind seeing her in her dirty underwear and looking her worst, you'd know it would be alright. He thought this very funny. But he also believed it, I think.

I was amused but didn't take it seriously. I mean, what sort of girl is going to risk being seen in her dirty knickers when she goes away for the first time with her boyfriend? What off the beam teacher told him this rubbish?

I must admit I'm not that fond of camping. In fact, I'm not all that keen on outdoor activities, full stop. But I put this aside because I wanted to be with Karl for longer than a day on our own, which is all we had had so far. And he was very keen we should camp together, so I did it for him. It crossed my mind to wonder how it would be if ever we set up together, him wanting to camp and fish and play rugby, and me not wanting any of that. But I pushed the thought away.

Anyway, as it happened we had fun and I enjoyed myself.

Until the crisis. I'm quite good at arranging things, I like having everything neat and exactly right, and Karl is the same. Karl isn't one of those boys, men, who have to be in charge all the time and have their way over everything. He takes pride in what he does, he's careful, he's amazing at paring what you need down to the essentials, and packing everything. He knew I'm not an experienced camper (to say the least). He discussed everything with me. And he tried to make sure we took what would make me comfortable, even if he didn't think it essential. The only thing we almost had a row about was the books I wanted to take and what Karl called my "stationery"—notebooks, pens, pencils, etc.—to which I am addicted and without which my life is unliveable. I countered by pointing out the amount of stuff he was taking for fishing. In the end, we came to an agreement, both of us cutting down to manageable amounts for carrying. But one thing I learned from this was how stubborn he can be. I had to be really firm before he agreed.

Not that we needed to, because my dad drove us to the place we were camping. It was where you spent a day with Karl, he told me. This also annoyed me when I found out, which I didn't till we were there. We could have taken a lot more stuff, but for Karl, Dad driving us was just luck, and we should only take what we could carry if we had to walk, otherwise, he said, it wasn't camping, it was setting up house.

As it turned out, it's just as well we did as he wanted.

We were lucky with the weather. There were showers in the night a couple of times, and a morning of rain. But I didn't mind the showers because they freshened everything. And though I'm not keen on camping, I have to admit I found there is something relaxing, and romantic as well, about being in a good rainproof tent, and the smell the rain brings out of the earth and the plants, and the feeling of being secure but very close to nature is really beautiful.

During the day Karl fished for hours on end. I knew

he had amazing concentration. I'd noticed this when we played chess. But I didn't know he had such stamina as well. Not that this was a problem, because I'm pretty good at concentrating for longish periods myself. I read a lot while he was fishing and also worked on an essay for school.

The first three days were pretty idyllic. One reason Karl said he wanted us to go away together was that he thought he'd be able to tell me all the things I wanted to know about him, because he'd be relaxed, and we'd have time, and he could do it better by telling me than writing it. I didn't remind him of this during those first three days. I thought it would be best to let him settle in and enjoy himself.

Now I have to tell you something I'd rather not, but it's part of what happened. It's about sex. When Karl and I got together both of us had already lost our virginity. But the first times hadn't been satisfactory for either of us. And neither of us had done any more. So we weren't exactly innocent, but we weren't what you'd call experienced either. Really, we learned about it together. What's for sure is we never enjoyed it so much as during those first three days and nights. But love isn't only about someone's sex, is it? There are more important things about a person than that.

So the first three days went by without us talking about Karl. But on the fourth day, because there was rain in the morning, we stayed in the tent and snuggled together and

I decided it was a good time to talk about the things I wanted him to tell me.

I asked him again why he found it so difficult to write answers to my questions. I said I'd liked his emails. Why couldn't he go on writing them.

He got all tensed up at that, and sat up.

I asked him what was the matter? What had I said that upset him?

He wouldn't reply. He closed himself off. The sudden contrast with the way he'd been, from relaxed and loving to silent and hard, hurt me and made me nervous.

I knew before that week he could be moody. Sometimes he would be full of fun and energy and playful and all over me. At other times he would be quiet and wanted to be still and serious. I didn't know why he was like that but was used to it and didn't mind. But this was different.

I tried to soothe him. I said whatever it was it didn't matter. We didn't have to talk about those things that day, if he didn't want to. But he wouldn't give, wouldn't look at me, didn't want me to hold him. He'd never been like that before.

I didn't know what to do. I felt like crying but made myself not. I couldn't stay lying down. I wanted to move around. But the tent was too small to stand in and the rain put me off from going out.

I sat up. We sat side by side, cross-legged, not looking at each other.

After a while he said he hadn't written the emails.

Just like that. No warning. Straight out.

I thought I must have heard wrongly. But he repeated it. "I didn't write the emails."

I said I didn't understand and asked him what he meant.

It was then he told me about coming to see you and how you'd written the emails for him.

It was one of those times when you can't believe what you're hearing. One part of you does, but another part doesn't. You feel confused, half shocked and half numb.

I said something about how could he do that? How could he deceive me like that? But it was as if someone else inside me was saying this.

He kept saying he was sorry, he hadn't meant to deceive me, he'd done it because he was afraid he'd lose me if he didn't write the answers well enough to please me.

I kept repeating how could he do that? Why did he think I'd not like what he'd written?

He didn't say anything about his dyslexia. He'd never mentioned this and he didn't then. If he'd told me I would have understood. Of course I would. But he didn't. And the longer it went on the more upset I became as what he was telling sunk in and all of me, not just a part, was upset so much I couldn't bear it anymore.

I pushed my way out of the tent. I was in floods of tears. I ran from the tent till I was far enough away for Karl not to hear me sobbing. Then I stood and let the rain fall on me, soaking me to the skin.

It was so cold it shocked me out of the shock.

I liked that it was so cold. I liked that it took the heat out of me. I liked that it was fresh. I liked that it wasn't people, just water. Unthinking, unfeeling, impersonal and water.

I don't know how to put this, but it was the first time in my life that I'd felt the comforting pleasure of dispassion. (Is dispassion a word?)

Whatever.

I stood there till I'd come to my senses.

Then I went back to the tent.

Inside, it seemed stuffy, smelt of our sweaty bodies, damp sweat from the rainy air.

Karl was sitting where I'd left him.

I undressed, towelled myself, and pulled on some clothes.

I sat facing him this time, and said how upset I was by what he'd told me, and couldn't understand why he'd done it. There must be something that would explain it.

I was guessing. It just felt like there must be.

It was then he told me about being dyslexic. It came out in fits and starts, like someone trying to sick up something stuck in his throat.

He told me how much he hated it, how it didn't matter what anyone said, experts saying you're gifted with dyslexia because it's supposed to make you able to think in ways people who aren't dyslexic can't, how it made you more creative, it was all rubbish. All he knew, he said, was that it had caused him trouble all his life. It had stopped him doing as well as he'd wanted to at school.

Once he got going it was like he couldn't stop. It poured out of him without any fits and starts and not even a pause for me to say anything. He told me how they found out that he was dyslexic, and what they did to try and help, and how the other kids treated him, and the whole story up till now. He told me how the only person who understood properly how he felt and who never treated him as odd or different or a worry or like a patient or in any way at all but as himself was his father. Not even his mother, only his father. He said he was getting on well by the time he went to secondary school, because of the support of his father, and how his father had taught him so much and all the things he loved doing, like fishing, chess, rugby, music, handcraft things, even cooking. And how that came to an end when his father died. After that he'd gone back to feeling like he used to. He explained how becoming a plumber had helped because he was good at it and the guy he was apprenticed to, who was his father's best friend, didn't care a toss about the dyslexia. He told me how he felt about me, which I won't repeat here, and how happy he'd been since we got together. Which is why he was worried about my questions and not writing the answers well enough and why he came to you. He said you'd been a bit like his father, you'd treated him as himself and as an equal and that he'd begun to value your friendship, not only because you'd helped him. He'd been happy again, he said, and now he'd wrecked it.

He didn't ask me to forgive him, but I knew that was what he meant. How could I not? I was still upset. But now I was annoyed with you, not him. I could see why he'd come to you. He was desperate. But you should have known it was wrong for him to send emails you'd written. You could have persuaded him to tell me about the dyslexia.

Well, anyway. We talked. I told him I understood. And I could see what he wanted wasn't words, but for me to show him it was alright between us. So by the end of the morning we were making love again.

The rest of that day we got back to the way we'd been before. But better. It was as if an invisible barrier between us had been removed. I hadn't realised it had been there. Now we both felt completely free with each other in a way we hadn't been before.

The rain cleared. The sun came out. We cleaned up, had something to eat. That afternoon we went for a long walk by the river. It was bliss.

When we got back Karl fished for a couple of hours while I read and worked on my essay. But I felt so happy, so relaxed, so in love that I couldn't do anything really except look at Karl standing in the river casting his line. He caught a couple of nice trout that he cooked and we ate for our evening meal.

We slept that night better than any before.

I was woken by Karl at dawn. There was just enough light filtering into the tent for me to see him. I have to explain that he had woken me each day at that time to make love, because he liked it best then. Afterwards we'd go to sleep again. I won't say I didn't like it because I did, but for Karl it was a special time and he was always urgent then.

That morning he was more urgent than I'd ever known him to be. He was, I mean he is, very strong. But he was always tender and thoughtful of me. I liked that. But that morning he was, let's say vigorous.

I'm not going to tell you what happened then because it is too private. All I'll say is I panicked. I was so scared I had to get away.

Suddenly it was as if he'd been switched off. He sort of slumped. Almost like he'd been knocked out.

I didn't know what to do. I said his name but he didn't respond. I pulled on my clothes. And sat facing him again.

His eyes were blank.

I said, I can't deal with this. I made some breakfast, trying to act normal, but he wouldn't eat any of it and neither could I. He just sat there like he was paralysed.

I waited for ages. An hour. Two. I don't know. All I know is I got more and more upset and more and more worried, him in the tent, me outside feeling cold and damp and horrible.

And that was it. I felt I couldn't go on. It was too much for me. So I decided to pack up and go.

When I told Karl all he said was, Do whatever you want.

I started putting my things together. Karl got his fishing gear and went off to the river without even saying good-bye or anything. I finished packing, cleared up in the tent and the cooking things, made everything as tidy as I could. And left.

There wasn't a mobile signal where we camped. As soon as I got one I phoned home. Luckily, Mum was in. She came and collected me from a pub in the nearest village.

All I told her and Dad was that it hadn't gone too well, Karl and I had had a row and I thought it best to break it off. Dad was pleased. He had nothing against Karl personally but thought I could do a lot better and it was too soon to get serious with anyone with university coming up.

Mum was more sympathetic. First love, she said, doesn't usually last, but I'd always remember it with affection. She told me about her first love, and Dad's. That helped. But didn't get rid of the hurt and the confusion. I just couldn't understand why Karl had acted the way he did. But I was too embarrassed to tell even my mother about that part.

I don't know why I've told you. And I haven't told you the worst part. I'm trusting you to keep all this to yourself. I hope you won't let me down this time. Let's say it's my gift to you in return for what your books have meant to me. Only there's a big difference. This isn't like your stories. It isn't fiction. It's fact.

TWELVE

I DIDN'T THEN AND WON'T NOW INDULGE IN THE POTTED psychology that might explain Karl's behaviour. What I did spend time brooding about was whether in anything Fiorella had told me there was a clue to how I might get in touch with him, but nothing came to mind.

I hate being unable to solve a puzzle. It nags like a persistent pain, disabling any other occupation. I tussled with myself all day. I asked myself what I'd do if this were one of my novels. What would I do at this point to push the plot on? But after trying this idea and that and each time being defeated by crumbling logic, every move lacking truth-to-life conviction, I accepted that this real-life problem couldn't be solved as if it were fiction, because in a novel I'd go back and change the plot so the stalemate would be avoided. But real life evolves its own unpredictable plots over which we characters have little control and only by hindsight, if then, discern the reasons and purposes.

The plain unwelcome fact is that sometimes life stymies you.

That day was one of those that seem to pass without the sun. I went to bed in querulous mood and spent another tussled night.

At eight thirty-five the next morning Mrs. Williamson phoned.

She wanted to know if Karl was with me. He'd been very low the night before. After she got up, she went to his room to see if he was all right, but his bed hadn't been slept in. She was worried that he might do something—

She didn't finish the sentence and didn't need to.

I asked if he might have gone to work.

She said she'd phoned his boss, but Karl wasn't with him. Then she thought of me.

I asked if Karl had taken anything—money, extra clothes, anything.

She said he hadn't.

I asked if she had called the police.

She said not yet.

I suggested she should.

She began to cry.

I could tell she was desperate and beginning to panic.

I asked whether it would be any help if I came over.

She said would I, please.

The police were helpful but not urgent. Hundreds—thousands—of people go missing every year. Most of them turn up somewhere, if not back at home. Some are never heard of again. A few, comparatively, suffer violent ends inflicted on themselves or by others. Karl, they said, was over eighteen, even though by only a few months, and so was legally an adult, responsible for himself. Even if they found him, they had no power to bring him home or even tell his mother where he was unless he wanted them to. If Mrs. Williamson had any evidence that Karl was a risk to himself or the public, or that he was in danger, in which case they would launch an inquiry, the best they could do was put his name on the missing persons list, and if Mrs. Williamson had a recent photo of Karl they'd add that to the file.

This did nothing to calm Mrs. Williamson's nerves. And I must admit I was worried too, though I tried not to show it.

Best to be practical, to do something.

I asked Mrs. Williamson to look again for anything Karl might have taken with him. But she said nothing was missing. His mobile phone was in his room. He never went anywhere without it. His keys and his wallet with money in it were there too. I wondered if he might have gone fishing. But his tackle was where he kept it in the spare bedroom.

Then it occurred to me. Was he on foot or on his bike?

His bike was kept in the garage. It wasn't there.

Mrs. Williamson had had no breakfast. I suggested she eat something while we took stock. She wouldn't eat but made coffee for us, which we drank while talking over the possibilities.

Karl had taken his bike but nothing else, nothing that suggested he had anything in mind—like buying something or going somewhere for a day out—nothing except going somewhere farther than even a longish walk. Unless he just wanted to cycle round for a while. But why? For exercise after being sedentary for days? A change of scene, when he hadn't been out for weeks? To meet someone, when he'd been unwilling to see anyone for months?

Any or all of those.

Or to transport himself far enough away to need his bike to get there quicker than by walking, somewhere he needed to go for a purpose brewed up by his self-tormenting melancholia.

And then a clue.

I asked Mrs. Williamson to have another look round Karl's room. This time she noticed that a photo of Karl's father wasn't on the table he used as a desk, and wasn't in any of the drawers or anywhere she looked. "I don't understand why I didn't notice it was gone before."

I remembered how, during the worst time of depression after Jane died, I'd thought about suicide. During the hours staring at the walls I planned where I would do it, and when, and how, so that there would be as little clearing up to do as possible by whoever found my body. I wrote letters apologising for causing distress.

Even as I planned this, I knew that thoughts of suicide were normal when you were melancholic. What's more, the antidepressants caused this as well.

I also remembered that when I was planning my death, I didn't want to do it at home because it would have seemed a violation. I chose a favourite haunt of ours. Quiet, off the beaten track, a good place to die, while remembering happy times with the person I loved beyond all description.

Not everyone would think like that. But if I was right about Karl, about the causes of his behaviour with Fiorella and his depression, I could imagine he might.

And I knew something else. I'd intended to hold a picture of my wife so that this would be the last thing I'd see while dying.

Was this what Karl meant to do? It did look frighteningly like it.

I mentioned none of this to Mrs. Williamson.

Life is not like a novel, but a novel can be like life. The best ones always are.

And I thought to myself, if I were writing the story of this moment in Karl's life, there was one place he'd go, whether planning to kill himself or only to wallow in his own pain.

It might seem odd to talk of someone wallowing in pain, but I knew from my experience that people obtain a strange pleasure from their suffering. In depression, you're keenly aware of every shift and shimmer of your body, every flicker and twinge of your feelings, every twist and turn of your thoughts, every fantasising image conjured by your imagination. You are all there is. You are all that matters. No one else, nothing else, has any meaning or importance, only yourself. In the deepest depths you are as high as on the strongest narcotics. And you can loll in that solipsistic paradise for days, months, even years, without requiring unreliable chemicals to keep you there. It's a self-generated, self-inflicted addiction, the cure of which only you can provide. The cure is called hope.

I explained to Mrs. Williamson where I thought Karl might be, but not why. As the desperate are, she was ready to cling to any hope of relief.

While I packed the Rover with the things I might need, she made some sandwiches and a flask of coffee, and insisted on including enough fruit and chocolate to last a week ("Karl loves chocolate"), bottles of soft drinks, a couple of cans of beer, as well as Karl's medication and a first aid box.

I made sure she had my mobile number and I hers, agreed with her that she would call me at once if there was any news, as I would her, and after receiving a hug and a tearful litany of thanks, drove off at precisely ten o'clock.

THIRTEEN

HE WAS THERE.

And he was alive.

I stopped, hidden among the trees a hundred metres or so from him. I could hardly stand for relief.

The glade by the river where we'd spent the crisp early spring day, and where he'd camped with Fiorella in the heat of summer, was gemmed in cool golden autumn, the trees moulting their leaves.

I'd parked in the lay-by and walked the ten-minute trek down the wooded valley as quietly as I could. I didn't want him to hear me in case he did something desperate before I could reach him.

My first thought was to let Mrs. Williamson know. But I remembered there wasn't a signal, though I checked to make sure. I didn't want to go back to the road, where there was one, for fear that Karl might do something untoward or leave before I got back.

When I first saw him, he was standing, head down, on the edge of the riverbank. Was he preparing to throw himself in? I took off the backpack so I'd be ready to rescue him. But after a few moments he walked a couple of steps, picked up a rock big enough to need two hands to lift it, which he carried a few steps from the river to a pile of stones about knee high. He placed the stone carefully on top, stood back and surveyed the pile, then returned to the river and stood again, head down for a few moments, before picking up another stone from the water's edge and carrying it to the pile.

This back-and-forth business went on long enough to build the pile up to his chest height, forming a roughly shaped pyramid-like mound, wide at the bottom, tapering to a flat top. It reminded me of the cairns that mark the highest points and sacred sites on the Yorkshire moors where I'd hiked in my youth.

I began to worry about what I'd do if this went on all day. I was already feeling cold—the autumn air among the trees in the bottom of the valley was chill with damp. My old man's settled ways had been upset by the events of the morning, breakfast was four hours ago and I'd not had my mid-morning coffee because I'd driven nonstop from Karl's house (breaking the speed limit wherever I dared, I have to confess). In the backpack were the coffee and sandwiches Mrs. Williamson had made. But they were intended for Karl more than me.

How long had I been hiding here? Going on an hour.

Time to make a move. I'd decompose into compost if I stayed much longer.

Making as if I were just arriving, I broke cover, walked to the river as if unaware of Karl, and sat myself down in a patch of sunlight on the edge of the riverbank ten metres or so from where he was standing, head down, looking into the water.

I opened the backpack, took out the flask and box of sandwiches, poured a mug of coffee, drank it, opened the box, took out a sandwich and began to eat.

It was hard not to glance at Karl, but I managed to keep my eyes to myself.

I took my time with this performance, a spur-of-the-moment, unthought improvisation, inspired by the basic need to eat and drink and warm up. The gentle autumn sun on my face and the refreshing ripple of the river at my feet raised my spirits.

Again I was going on my own experience of melancholia. It had helped to have a sympathetic friend with me, so long as they didn't talk much, and didn't ask about how I was feeling and why and offer suggestions for "getting better." Silent companionship, yes. Fuss and advice, no.

I'd finished one sandwich when Karl came and sat down

beside me. I pushed the sandwich box towards him. He took a sandwich and began to eat. I poured a mug of coffee and set it down near him. I helped myself to a second sandwich and ate it. He too, after drinking his coffee. I refilled both our mugs. When the sandwiches were finished—five for him, two for me—I held the bar of chocolate out to him. He took it and set to work eating it.

I studied the view—the river dappled and ribbled with sunlight, the harlequin autumn trees rising up the valley opposite.

Karl finished the chocolate.

"How did you know?" he said to his feet.

"Guesswork," I said to the river. "It's what I'd have done."

"Liked lurking about behind that tree, did you?"

I smiled to myself. "Never much good at the scouting lark," I said.

I packed away the box and flask.

"Your fishing gear is in the car," I said.

"If you like."

"Want to come with me to get it?"

"I'm OK here."

"I thought you might want to let your mother know you enjoyed her sandwiches."

"I would, but I forgot my mobile."

"Mind if I do?"

"Please yourself."

"I'll be as quick as I can."

"No rush."

We looked at each other for the first time.

He gave me a down-turned smile. "I'm not going anywhere."

A risk. A test of my trust. And trust dies from ifs and buts.

I was back in thirty minutes. It had taken a ten-minute call to Mrs. Williamson to give her time to vent her relief and to reassure her that Karl was all right, that I'd not leave him, would take care of him whatever happened, and get him home as soon as he'd agree. She wanted to know why he'd left without telling her, and what he was doing. I had to tell her I didn't know and thought it best for Karl to explain when he felt he wanted to, that there was no use questioning him, it would only dam him up and even turn him away. I could hear in her voice as she rang off—"Give him all my love, tell him I'm here for him anytime"—that her relief was tangled with the anxiety of absence.

When I got back, Karl was busy piling more stones onto his cairn. He stopped when I arrived and again we sat side by side contemplating the view, his fishing tackle lying between us.

Coffee is, for the old, a potent diuretic. After twenty minutes or so I had to make for the trees. When I returned, Karl was assembling his rod.

"Anything left in the sandwich box?" he asked.

I opened it. He took some cheese, nipped off a small knob, rubbed it into a ball between his fingers, and threaded a hook through it on the end of the line.

"Not fly-fishing today?"

He shook his head.

"Will they go for that?"

"On a good day some coarse fish go for anything. Bread, bits of meat, cheese. Cupboard bait."

There was a backwater pool under a tree a few metres away. Karl cast his line into it, and remained sitting, rod in hand, eyes on the float.

During the next hour or so—for once I didn't check my watch—he caught nothing, now and then wound in his line, renewed the bait, and cast again.

But that was only displacement activity, keeping his hands busy while he did something else, something that I could tell took all his will power against the resentful passion of his melancholia.

What he did was talk. Not the fluent flow of the time at this very spot when he told me about his love of fishing, but in gobs squeezed out of his mouth, expectorations of words and phrases, sometimes a few sentences together. It was as if one part of him was trying to speak while the other part tried to strangle the words before he could say them.

To write down what he said in the tormented fashion in which it was spoken—I've tried to do it—is as tortuous to read as it was to hear and for Karl to utter. So instead

I've composed his monologue—which it mostly was, because I interrupted only to ask a question now and then—into a continuous speech that accurately honours, I hope, his meaning, and uses his own words as far as I recall them—which isn't difficult because Karl's declaration was so unsparing of himself and so trusting of me that I shall remember it for the rest of my life.

FOURteen

Karl's Declaration

I meant to do it.

I came here to do it.

I'd worked out how.

I'd thought about it for days.

Nights as well.

I didn't sleep much.

Planned it.

Went over and over it in my mind.

Didn't want to do it at home because of Mother. Took
as long as I did to decide to do it because of her. Thinking
what it would do to her.

But it kind of built up in me.

The more I thought of doing it the harder it got not to
do it and the less I thought of Mother or anybody else.

By the time I decided last night I wasn't thinking about anybody except myself.

I didn't care about anybody anymore.

I just wanted to end the pain.

What pain? What caused it?

Don't know.

Hard to say.

Fiorella.

She dumped me.

And what I did then.

The way I behaved.

That started it.

And Dad.

It brought him back.

Not having him.

Him not being here.

It all got mixed up.

My fault about Fiorella.

Don't know what came over me.

Why? What did you do?

Doesn't matter.

It did her in and she dumped me.

And then it all came over me.

Like it had been waiting to happen for ages.

Well—since my dad.

I don't know.

It was like sliding down into a deep pit, a deep dark place, and I couldn't stop myself. Down and down. Leaving everything behind.

Even myself.

Like I wasn't me anymore.

Like a fish when you've gutted it and what's left when you've eaten the good bits. The bones. The carcass.

I felt like that.

A carcass.

But still alive.

I did struggle.

I did try.

But the longer it went on the harder it got.

Like I'd been drugged with poison.

Sapped my energy.

I'd lost everything. Even myself.

And there wasn't any hope of ever getting any of it back again.

Not even myself.

Or of getting out of the pit.

Never getting anything right again.

[*He went on like this for quite a while, going over and over how he'd felt, as if repeating it was the only way to understand it—to try to understand himself. Until finally I said:*]

You felt lost.

Lost?
Everything lost.
Whatever.
Anyway, it got too much.
Couldn't stand it anymore.
Just wanted it to stop.
That's what happened last night.
Couldn't take it anymore so I came here to do it.

Why here?

D'you believe in life after death?

No.

No. Nor me neither.
Dad didn't.
He used to say what is *is* and you'll know what is when
it happens.
And he said the people who say they know are the worst.
But do you believe anything of you stays behind?

I don't know.

Nor me neither.
But I've never felt Dad has gone.

I mean, sometimes I feel if I turn round he'll be there. Not him like he was. I mean, not . . . well . . . flesh and blood. But him. Somehow him. Him. There.

Have you ever felt that about somebody?

Yes.

Who?

My wife.

Your wife?

She's dead.

You never said.

No.

I wondered.

Because she was never there when I came to see you and you never mentioned her.

Well, anyway.

The thing is, Dad loved this place.

We had the best time here.

Since he went I've tried not to think too much about him.

Can't help it, though.

And feeling he was still there, still here somehow. I thought if I came back it might help.

That's why I came here with you.

I didn't want to do it on my own and not with Mother.

And coming here with you and, you know, the thing with the memory stick. It was good. I liked it.

And because there was Fiorella.

And you'd been like—

Well, you'd been a help.

I was feeling so good. Fit and well. Really fit and really well for the first time since Dad went. I thought I must be getting over it, must be accepting it, because I hadn't yet.

I see that now.

So bringing Fiorella here was a kind of celebration.

If you want to put it like that.

A celebration of Dad.

And a celebration of Fiorella and me.

I didn't tell her that.

Maybe I should have.

Maybe she'd have understood.

I thought it would be great, really good.

This morning, when a lot of this stuff has come clear, I saw I was kind of bringing Fiorella to meet Dad, to show her off to him.

Does that sound daft?

No. It sounds true.

And it was like that at first.

For three days it was like that.

And nights.

Nights like I'd never imagined nights could be.

I've never been so happy.

Maybe I was too happy.

Can you be too happy?

Maybe you can. Maybe when you're too happy you believe whatever you want is possible. Everything can be the way you want it to be. Nothing can stop you.

That's what I felt here with Fiorella.

You know what I mean?

What I'm saying?

I know what you mean.

I'd never had it like that before.

I don't mean just the sex. But, you know, all of it, the two of us alone in the night.

It was like everything came together then, all of me.

You know?

I know.

My body, my mind, all my feelings, all my thoughts.

All of me.

And I think it was the same for her.

I know it was.

She said it was.

And it was when we were together like that is when it happened.

What? . . .
What happened?

Like a wave.

Like a tidal wave.

Like a tsunami, rushing up like I was a boat on the wave, carried on the wave, not able to stop or change direction.

Not that I wanted to. No no!

It was good, it was so, *so* good!

And while it was happening this stuff started coming out of my mouth.

About having a baby.

About wanting us to have a baby.

About starting it right then . . .

I don't know where it came from.

It was me. But it wasn't me saying it.

I was out of it.

Out of my head.

Out of myself.

I was gone.

But I was all here as well.

All there.

Wanting us to have a baby . . .

I tried to make her.

Make her let me . . .

She got scared.

I didn't mean to scare her.

But she got scared.

And made me stop.

And then I felt so—

Shocked.

With myself.

I couldn't speak.

Couldn't look at her.

Ashamed.

[*He was panting, almost hyperventilating. Sweat covered his face. His eyes were big and staring. I felt he was seeing himself, observing himself, as he had been at that moment, and at the same time he was experiencing it again, and he was amazed by himself.*

He stopped and said nothing for a while, until the fit had passed and he was calm again.]

Anyway, that was it.

She couldn't take it.

I frightened her.

She dumped me.

I tried to get her back.

Phoned her to say sorry and explain.

But she wouldn't talk to me.

Her mother answered.

I don't think she ever liked Fiorella going with me.

I know her father didn't.

She said Fiorella didn't want to speak to me or see me ever again and I should leave her alone.

That's when the slide started.

Couldn't get her out of my mind.

Couldn't give her up.

And that's when I started fretting about Dad again.

And it got so bad I couldn't go to work.

I didn't want to go to work.

I didn't want to do anything or see anybody.

Couldn't leave my room.

I knew I was worrying Mum sick. But it was like I was stuck in mud. All the energy sucked out of me.

I could hardly move.

Spent the day staring at the walls doing nothing, the same thoughts, the same feelings sloshing around inside me like blocked-up plumbing that's gone wrong.

Maybe it had. Maybe the plumbing in your mind had gone wrong.

You mean I'd gone crazy?

I tell you, thinking about it now, it does seem like I was crazy.

This morning I feel like I've just come out of the loony bin.

But I didn't feel crazy at the time.

The plumbing might be dodgy but not my thoughts.

My body felt pretty grotty, but everything I was thinking seemed logical.

As logical as a game of chess, every move planned, and the aim clear.

I'd lost Dad.

I'd lost Fiorella.

[*He chuckled. A bitter sound.*]

The king and the queen both out of the game!

And there wasn't a hope in hell of getting them back.

So I'd lost.

Why go on?

Time to end it.

But you haven't.

No.

What stopped you?

When I was thinking about it.

All those hours.

I was thinking about how to do it.

Looked it up on the internet.

One site listed all the ways. But it said, if you mess it up, you end up a basket case. A vegetable. Still alive but worse off than before and not able to do anything about it.

For the best ways, the surest ways, I didn't have the gear.

Like a gun or poison that worked in seconds.

But even if I had, nothing like that seemed right.

I wanted to do it somehow that seemed right.

Does this sound silly?

I mean, it's like choosing the right fishing gear, or a car, or, I dunno, anything. You want what suits you.

Well, it was like that.

Another site had examples of the way some famous people had done it.

And there was one, a famous writer, the way she did it I knew was the right way for me.

Everything sort of came together then.

I knew the place, and the place had what I needed for the way I wanted to do it.

I think I know the writer who you mean. Water and stones.

I love water. Always have. Dad too. He taught me to swim when I was a baby. So young I don't even remember.

But if I chucked myself into the river I wouldn't be able to stop myself from swimming.

So I was going to fill my backpack with heavy stones, and tie some to my hands and feet.

The pile on the bank.

That's how it started.

But there's a lot more than you'd need.

[*He smiled. A first since I'd arrived. But still didn't look at* me.]

How come?

It was dawn when I got here.
Enough light to see by.
Started looking for stones.
They had to be right as well.
Exactly right.
Right shape. Right look.
Have you noticed the stones in the water by the bank?
All sizes and shapes and colours.
In the water they look so bright. So fresh.
Like gems.
I thought it would be easy to find what I wanted.
But it wasn't.
I put the first one on the bank.
Then the next.
Then another.
I kept going because I kept thinking I might find one better than the others.

Then it got to be like I couldn't stop.

It was like when I'm fishing.

You know?

Concentrated, absorbed, you forget everything. Time. Other people.

The pile got higher and higher.

And then it got so big it got top heavy and fell over.

Collapsed.

I didn't like that.

It was a mess.

I hate messes.

So I started again.

But this time I kind of planned it.

Made a square of bigger stones, bigger than I'd need except for the base.

When I'd laid the base, like a platform, I had a thought.

I'd brought a photo of Dad to have with me when I did it.

But now I thought I'd bury it in the pile of stones.

A memorial.

Sort of.

Yes. A memorial.

I think I still meant to do it.

But I wanted to build this memorial to Dad and him and me being here.

This time it took a lot longer than before.

For each layer I had to have the right size and shape of stones, getting smaller towards the top, to make the thing solid and stable.

I needed a lot more stones as well.

So I kept going.

And you know what?

What?

I started to enjoy it.

And the more I went on, the better I wanted it to be, and the better I made it, the more I enjoyed it.

I kept undoing what I'd done and redoing it better.

With better stones from the river for each layer.

And that's when you turned up.

[*He chuckled again. Smiled again. Looked at me.*]

Lurking in the trees.

Which you are no good at!

Can't tell you how relieved I was when I saw you.

I hadn't finished when I saw you.

I was still going to do it.

But then I saw you.

And I wasn't.

[*He turned away.*

Stood up.

Took up his rod, which he'd laid down on the ground before he started his declaration, and wound in the line.

Nothing on the hook. Not even the bait.

He chuckled again at this.

I waited for him to say some more. There was so much more I wanted to know.

But he said nothing and I sensed he'd said all he was going to say today.]

[*I stood up.*

He put his hand into a pocket, took it out, turned to me, holding out his hand, which was clasping something.

He waited a moment, then opened his hand.

Lying in the palm was a small rust-red stone, about the size of my thumbnail.

It was smooth and round, with flat sides.

And there was a hole through the middle.

Like a very small doughnut.

I couldn't tell whether it was natural. Or the hole was man-made.]

For you.

Why? What is it?

A present.
Take it.

[*I took it. It was unexpectedly heavy for its size.*]

Thank you.

[*I was at a loss for any other words.*]

Give us a hand to finish.

[*He turned away and walked to the stone pile, the memorial.
I pocketed my present and followed him.*]

FIFteen

- - - - - - -

WE FINISHED BUILDING THE CAIRN WITHOUT MUCH BEING SAID, except of a practical sort—which stones to use; how to construct the cairn so that it was stable and solid—the photo of his father buried at its heart.

Karl was concentrated, as if all the emotions of his declaration were absorbed into the stones and his attention to our work.

By the time we were done the cairn looked sufficiently monumental for anyone who came across it to see it was more than merely a pile of stones. About a metre square at the base, it stood a metre and a half high, tapering to a flat top about thirty centimetres square, which we capped with a slab of slate just the right size that we'd found in the river.

We stood for a moment or two, side by side, looking at it.

I felt something should be said to mark the occasion, but couldn't think of anything appropriate.

Then we washed our hands and faces in the river, collected our belongings, and strolled in single file, Karl leading the way, up to the car. We retrieved Karl's bike from the hedge where he'd hidden it and stowed it in the back of the Rover. And then I phoned Mrs. Williamson to let her know we were on our way.

By now I was feeling the pinch. My old man's energy wasn't up to such unrelenting activity and emotional ups and downs. And the long drive, without a stop, and the shifting of heavy stones had set off the sciatica. The last thing I felt like doing was drive the car back home. I'd supposed Karl would do this, but he climbed into the passenger seat without a word, and by the time I'd phoned his mother and eased into the driver's seat, he was fast asleep, out like a light and dead to the world.

I had to stop three times to walk about, rest my back, and consult the hedgerows. Karl never woke, never moved during the entire journey.

When we got back, Mrs. Williamson, not knowing whether to laugh or cry, did both simultaneously. The prodigal son responded as best he could, but all he wanted was to go to bed. His mother urged food on him, a bath, a shower, a litany of questions about how he was and what he wanted ("Just bed, Mum, just bed"), and telling him how good I'd been and wasn't I clever to know where to find him.

All to no avail. Karl was in bed, unwashed, unfed and unconscious fifteen minutes after we arrived.

As for me, I wanted to be back in my own home and to attend to myself no less than Karl wanted his bed. But out of fellow feeling accepted Mrs. Williamson's offer of a meal while I gave her a brief report on what had happened, including the building of the cairn, but omitting Karl's declaration, which I knew would raise many questions to which I neither knew the answers nor had the stamina to discuss. I left her to nurse her relieved delight on her own as soon as I could, promising to phone later.

I felt a touch guilty, leaving her like that, but there are times when guilt is no rival to the need to save yourself.

When I phoned late that evening, Mrs. Williamson reported that Karl had slept until about six, then got up, showered, ate a meal of fried eggs and bacon, before going back to bed, where he still was, fast asleep. He'd said very little, except that he "felt a bit better" but was "knackered."

We agreed his fatigue was natural and understandable and was perhaps a good sign that he was recovering.

Mrs. Williamson, however, was as lively as a bumblebee, still buzzing with relief, gratitude and maternal desire to coddle her only child.

I promised I'd phone again next morning, which I did,

but not till midday. I, too, was knackered. To adapt the famous lines from the Remembrance Day poem, age does weary them, and the years do condemn those who live to be old. There is no escaping the deracination of time. I felt done in by the previous day's excursions. But the pain of revived sciatica prevented solid sleep. My joints ached, my limbs felt filleted of their bones, and I was urinating even more often than usual and with some pain. No position, standing, sitting or lying down, was comfortable for long. I'd been through this before, much worse, and knew that patience was the only cure for my body and listening to music the only salve for my soul. Exhaustion that would have needed no more than a good night's sleep for recovery only a few years ago, now required three or four.

This time when I phoned, Mrs. Williamson sounded as if she had tumbled down from yesterday's high and fallen into a slump. Karl, however, was up and in better shape than for some weeks. He was in the garden "pottering about," his mother said. Of course, he hadn't gone to work, too soon for that, if indeed he was on the mend, which it was also too soon to know. Mrs. Williamson was staying home from her job, because she was afraid to leave Karl alone "in case he relapsed." She was worried about being off work so much.

Had I felt up to it, I'd have offered to Karl-sit. But my resources of compassion were as weak as the rest of me. I said I'd help out tomorrow, which seemed to cheer her up.

I phoned early next morning, intending to be at Karl's in time for Mrs. Williamson to go to work as usual. But she said Karl wanted to be on his own, had persuaded her that he would be OK, wouldn't "do anything silly," and needed her to trust he'd "get himself back onto his feet." He had agreed that she could phone him whenever she wanted to. I asked her to tell Karl he could phone or come and see me at any time.

That day passed without a word from Karl. Mrs. Williamson phoned during her lunch break to tell me that Karl was pottering about in the garden, and again when she got home that afternoon, to tell me he was making another fly for his fishing.

Next day, the same calls, and the day after. The fourth day, Mrs. Williamson reported that Karl had cleared his room out and—for the next three days—was repainting it, the walls white, the woodwork the shade of blue, Karl had told his mother, of the song thrush's eggs.

Each day she sounded more cheerful and confident. But "we're not out of the wood yet," she added with a defensive caution against disappointment that I'd come to recognise was part of her nature.

And so as the days went by, I called less and less frequently, and so did Mrs. Williamson. It became clear that Karl was much better and improving in spirits all the time.

And though still not going to work, he was keeping himself busy at home and had started fishing again in the local river.

During that time my doctor arranged for me to see a consultant, who advised I might need a prostate operation in the next few months if the medication I was taking didn't show better results soon. Luckily, the condition was still in the early stages and, he suggested, could be dealt with without too much difficulty, the prognosis being good for a complete recovery.

This began to occupy me—by which I mean worry me—more than my concern for Karl. Of course, I didn't mention it to Mrs. Williamson, though there were moments when I had to resist a temptation to spill the beans. One of the problems of living on your own at my age, after more than forty years of married life, is having no one at home to talk to about your worries, no one who can shore up your confidence and cheer you up. Friends, however good and close, are not the same support as a loving partner, who knows you inside out.

A couple of weeks later Fiorella's name popped up in my message box.

Hi. I heard Karl is ill. Is he OK?

I asked who had told her.

His boss. He's doing some work in our house. What's wrong with Karl? Is it serious? His boss says it is.

It was. But he's getting better.

What was it?

It's not right for me to tell you.

That means it must be mental or emotional, because if he'd broken a leg or something physical was wrong, I think you'd tell me.

No comment.

Was it because of what happened between us?

No comment.

I bet it was. I wish you'd tell me because if it is I feel I'm to blame. Partly anyway.

I wouldn't say you're to blame.

So it is, isn't it? I'd like to see him.

I thought you'd broken up with him for good.

I did, but I can't forget him, can't get him out of my mind. Maybe what happened wasn't so bad. It frightened me and I panicked. I've thought a lot about it. I think I can see why he behaved like he did. He was all mixed up about his dad and me and not being able to write like I wanted him to. What do you think?

I don't know.

I think he needs me. I could help him get better. And I want to see him again. I'll try to.

Up to you, of course. But it wouldn't be a good idea just to turn up at his house unexpected.

Give me some credit.

Best of luck.

sixteen

|

A couple of weeks went by after that without anything more from either Karl or Fiorella.

Mrs. Williamson called every two or three days to keep me up to date—Karl was pretty much the same.

During the third week the good news was that Karl had gone back to work. Only part-time but a good sign. He found the first week hard going but stuck at it. Though he was still morose now and then, his mother felt he was at last on the mend.

Then, the following week, I had a phone call. The organiser of a weekend conference for teachers on the subject of teaching novels. They'd planned a talk by a famous author for Saturday after lunch, but she had cancelled because of a family crisis, and they wondered if I could "save their bacon." A very good fee was offered, all expenses paid, hotel accommodation if required. I was assured of the delightful nature of the location—a comfortable conference hotel in the Devon countryside—and of a hearty welcome from the hundred and fifty appreciative teachers. I suppose on the embarrassment-saving principle of "never explain, never apologise," nothing was said about why I hadn't been their first choice, or indeed how many other possible substitutes they'd approached before coming to me. But then, I didn't need to be told. I have no illusions that I am anything other than an author of minor importance, who enjoys, if that is the word, a devoted but small readership.

My first impulse was to refuse. I hate public speaking, probably because I'm not very good at it; I detest anything to do with selling myself or my books; I dislike socialising as the celebrity guest; and, to be frank, felt a bit miffed at being shochorned in as the last-minute replacement for the best-selling author everybody was expecting to meet.

But this impulse was stifled by—what? The seduction of vanity. Even as the understudy, at least I'd been invited, and however much you dislike yourself for it, flattery does work. More persuasive than that, the prospect of publicity. It's easier to write a book than sell it, as every publisher will readily tell you if you complain about your poor sales. And all of us in the word business know that authors meeting readers is the best way of selling their books. I've never understood why readers are so influenced by meeting writers. As a reader myself, it's the last thing I want to do. In my experience most writers of books you've admired are disappointing as people. How can it be otherwise? If they're any use as writers, the best of them will be in their books.

So, out of vanity and crude commercial judgement, I accepted. As there was no convenient rail service, I said I'd drive there on Saturday morning in time for lunch, and return home after my talk.

I regretted this as soon as I put the phone down. Had to restrain myself from phoning back and cancelling. But no. It would have been unprofessional.

To get me out of the house—an action that would quieten my troubled mind—I drove to the local petrol station and filled up and put the car through the washer—but knew by the time I got home, even from that short trip, I'd be crippled by sciatica after a two-and-a-half-hour drive, never mind the drive back. I could stay overnight to give myself a rest before driving home, but the thought of spending the evening with a crowd of teachers letting their hair down decided me against that solution. And though I could do it all in one day by train, I didn't fancy a long train journey with two changes. Besides, the weather was cold and grey, and all my instincts were urging me to hibernate.

Again I thought of cancelling. But dithered.

Then I thought of Karl. Perhaps he'd drive me. Perhaps he'd like a day out. And one more persuasion. Apparently there was a sculpture park in the extensive grounds of the hotel, which was bounded by a river offering "excellent trout fishing available to hotel guests." Ideal for Karl while I was at the conference—three or four hours at most, but enough perhaps to tempt him.

Which it did. We agreed to set off at eight on Saturday morning. When we got there, Karl would fish while I cavorted with the teachers, then set off home about four. Back by seven, traffic and weather permitting.

II

During the journey neither of us was talkative. I never am before a public appearance. My mind is all on what I'm going to say. My nerves are agitated by fear of failure. I'm withdrawn and irritable.

Karl was, I guess, regretful, wishing he'd refused. I knew from my own time in the pit of depression that you grow almost to enjoy your illness, even when it's at its worst, preferring to be shut away on your own, no one else to attend to but yourself, wallowing in the slough of your maundering condition, like a hippopotamus lolling about in a sticky slough of mud.

Needless to say, we had to stop after an hour for me to consult a hedge.

When I got back into the car, instead of driving on, Karl, staring ahead as if at something blocking the way, said,

"Why am I me?"

It took a moment to adjust my enclosed mind. "You mean, why are you you rather than someone else?"

"Why am I me? D'you ever wonder why you are you?"

"Doesn't everyone?"

"Do they? Does anyone know why?"

"I very much doubt it."

"You know how many people there are in the world?"

"Billions?"

"Very nearly seven billion. That's seven with nine noughts after it."

"Unimaginable." (And can we please get on?)

"Why am I not one of them and not me? Don't you think it's weird to be you and not someone else?"

"If anything's weird, the weird thing is being human."

A pause. No sign of getting on.

I said, "I thought you believed that what is *is* and that's all there is to it."

"I do normally."

"What do you mean, normally?"

"Before. I'm not normal now, am I? I haven't been normal for ages."

"You mean, since the crisis."

"Yes. When I was really bad, I mean the worst time. I couldn't stand being only me. And not knowing why. I wanted to stop being me. I just wanted to stop. I wanted not to be. I wanted to be nothing."

"And now you're over the worst?"

"Since at the river. Not wanting to get rid of myself. I do believe what is *is*. Only I keep wanting to know why. And I wish . . ."

"What?"

"I wish . . ."

"Wish what?"

"I don't know. I don't know how to say it. I don't know what I wish or how to say about being me and about why."

My mind was at sixes and sevens now, wanting to say something useful, but mainly wanting to think about this wretched talk, and get there, and get it done, and get back home, and so I said nothing, having nothing worth saying.

Karl waited a moment, before coming to, starting up and driving on.

The rest of the journey passed with only the occasional patch of talk, about the route, or the weather (fine, cold, cloudy, a couple of showers), or the countryside (winter setting in, the trees waiting for a final stormy blow to shed their remaining leaves).

Except that out of the blue Karl mentioned receiving an email from Fiorella, saying she'd heard from his boss he was off work ill, and asking how he was.

I asked whether he'd replied. He said he hadn't. I didn't ask why.

III

I won't describe my reception and performance at the conference. It has nothing to do with Karl. Except to say that afterwards, as usual, I felt a total failure, and suffered minor agonies of embarrassment about what I did say and how I said it, and what I didn't say and how I should have said it. Had I been on my own I'd have driven away at once and spent the journey in recovery by verbally flagellating myself for my ineptitude. But I had to find Karl and shift the gears of my mood from self-abusing sulks to at least a semblance of civility.

I walked down to the river but couldn't find him. No one else was around to ask if they'd seen him. The grounds of the hotel—once a stately home, it was even better than its publicity, a rare quality—were extensive, partly wooded, partly parkland. I didn't fancy trekking everywhere, on the hunt for him. In my disordered state of mind, I began to worry that he might after all have done something silly. I knew how easy it was to slip back into the pit while clawing your way out of it.

What to do?

Calm down, I told myself. Think sensibly.

Of course! Phone him! I took out my mobile and rang his number. Karl answered. Relief!

I said I was ready to go home, where was he? He said he was looking at something he'd like me to see and told me how to find him. He sounded excited, quite the opposite from his earlier moroseness, and the first time I'd heard that note in his voice since the crisis began.

As I've mentioned, the hotel included a "sculpture trail"—a path that wound through the grounds, with sculptures by many artists displayed here and there. Karl was in a glade in the wooded area, sitting on a bench, leaning forward, arms on thighs, hands clasped together—a posture I'd learned he adopted when thinking hard. He was gazing at what looked to me like a pile of loosely tangled metal rods perched on top of a block of grey stone.

He didn't budge when I sat down beside him, and only after a few moments of silence said,

"What d'you think?"

"What about?"

He nodded at the pile of rods.

"I don't know. Meant to be a sculpture, obviously."

"See how it's made?"

"Metal rods."

"Steel. And all one piece, no joins. One length of steel rod. Probably bent by the same kind of tool we use to make bends in pipes."

"Yes, I see. It flows quite attractively. Turning in on itself and out again. It looks a bit like a doodle drawn with a black pen."

"But in three-D."

"Yes, a three-D doodle."

Karl got up and walked round the sculpture, running

his hand along the rod, feeling its shape, then standing back to view it, here and there bending down to look at it from below. There was energy in his movements, vigour and concentration.

"It's different from every angle," he said. "You wouldn't think that something so simple could make such different shapes from different angles. And it's so good to look at, you can't help touching it."

He toured twice more before I said, "Maybe the artist—"

"William Tucker," Karl said, pointing to a label on the base. "And it's called *Beulah One*."

"I wonder what that means."

"No idea."

"Maybe it doesn't mean anything. Maybe it's only meant to be something pleasant to look at."

"You mean, it's just a . . . just a *thing* . . . End of story?"

"Why not? If you want to put it that way."

"A thing that pleased him."

"Like a poem, only made of a steel rod, not words."

Karl looked at me and smiled.

"I like that!" he said. "Poetry in steel. That's good!"

He sat down again.

"I've been looking at it for ages," he said. "And the more I look at it, the more I want to look at it."

We were silent for a while. But, as ever, I was aware of the time and wanted to be home because by now I was feeling cold and damp. If I stay much longer, I thought, I'll come down with a cold or my joints will seize up.

"Look," I said, "I hate to be a spoilsport, but I'd rather like to make for home, if you wouldn't mind."

He got up. But his eyes were still on the sculpture. He walked over to it and ran his hand along a curving section of it.

"I'm sorry," I said.

"No," he said, coming back to me, "it's OK."

We walked to the car and drove away.

"There was another," Karl said, when we'd settled into the journey. "By a different artist. It was made of rods as well. They were shaped into the outline of two people, a man and a woman, very tall, taller than real people. It's like they were drawn in the air. I saw that one first. Looked at it for ages."

He was like a man woken from a long sleep, and refreshed by breakfast.

"Did you do any fishing?" I asked.

"No. I thought I'd have a walk round, to stretch my legs after the drive, and have some coffee first. I saw some of the sculptures, which I quite liked. Hadn't seen anything like them before. Then came across the one of the man and woman outlined in steel rods. The others had been all right, but this one really impressed me. And the way it was made of bent rods welded together made me think of my job. So I sat on a bench near it and had some coffee and, I don't know, went on just sitting there for ages, looking at the sculpture, and thinking."

163

"Thinking what?"

"Nothing much."

"But thinking?"

"Not about anything really."

"Thoughtless thinking?"

"Thoughtless thinking?"

He gave me a quick glance, and we both laughed.

"Or maybe," I said, "letting your body do the thinking."

He stared at me, as if in surprise.

"Body thinking?" he said.

And broke into a fit of laughter, as if he had heard the best joke in the world. He was laughing so much he couldn't speak and had to stop the car till the fit wore off, when he said: "Yes. Body thinking. That's what I do."

I waited till he'd calmed down before saying, "And then?"

"Nothing. Sat there for I don't know how long. Meant to go back to the car for my gear, but must have turned the wrong way, because I got a bit lost. And then I came across the sculpture that really grabbed me. The other one was meant to be a man and a woman. But this one wasn't anything except, like you said, just a shape, just a *thing*. As soon as I saw it, I felt . . . well, I felt it was mine . . . That sounds stupid when I say it."

"Not stupid at all. I've felt that about a book. A novel."

"That it was yours? That it had been made only for you?"

"A long time ago. When I was young."

"Well, anyway, I couldn't help it. I just had to sit and look at it."

"And do some body thinking?"

"You could say. The others were made of various stuff. Wood and stone and concrete. But the man and woman and this *Beulah One* were made of nothing except some bent rods. They were as simple as you can get. But the more I looked at them, the more I got out of them. That's what I liked."

"So you're glad you came?"

"I'm glad I came, thanks. But, hey, I haven't asked how you got on. Was it OK?"

"Least said, soonest forgotten."

"As bad as that?"

"No. Not bad, not good. But that kind of carry-on isn't me."

"So what is you?"

"Words on paper. Reading them and writing them."

He grinned. "So all you are is words on paper?"

"Not quite. But when I'm on my own, reading and writing, I'm most myself and most at home with myself. And, by the way, I see we need some petrol. We'd better pull in at the next service station."

"Where, if my guess is right, you'll need to consult the hedge?"

"You're getting to know me too well, young man!"

seventeen

SOMETIMES I WONDER IF WE REALLY DO BRING UNPLEASANT things upon ourselves just because we say they might happen. Isn't that why we say "touch wood" or "don't speak too soon" or "don't count your chickens before they're hatched"?

Of course, it's all baloney, mere superstition. But still, when I came down with 'flu a couple of days after sitting too long in the cold and damp, I couldn't help thinking that if I hadn't thought of it then, it might never have happened.

Whatever, I woke on Monday morning as floppy as a wet rag, aching in every muscle and joint, sweating as if in a sauna, my nose feeling like it was full of frothy soap, and my eyes streaming.

They say the young have the ability but lack the wisdom, and the old have the wisdom but lack the ability.

A crudely true generalisation. That morning the wisdom of experience told me I had a bad case of the 'flu, but the inability of old age prevented me from doing much about it.

I took a couple of analgesic pills, drank some water and lay in bed bemoaning my bad luck.

I won't go on about the following forty-eight hours because they have nothing to do with Karl's story.

The next thing that happened, which does, was a phone call from Mrs. Williamson on the Thursday evening. (For those who, like myself, keep track of time, this was five days after the trip.)

The reason she called wasn't mentioned because as soon as she heard my voice she asked if I was all right. I replied as hypocritically as I could that I had "a bit of a cold."

"You sound dreadful," she said, which cheered me up at once.

"No, no," I said. "I'm fine."

"No, you aren't," she said. "How long have you been like this?"

"Since Monday. But it's nothing to fuss about."

"I expect you picked it up on Saturday, talking to all those people. Some of them were bound to be full of cold. There's a lot of it about."

The usual dialogue on such occasions then followed, including an interrogation into whether I was up or in bed (in bed), who was looking after me (myself), was I drinking a lot of liquids, especially fruit juice (yes: a lie; honest answer: very little, because I was too weak to bother), what had I eaten (cornflakes, toast and marmalade), how often (enough; untrue: once), what was I taking (analgesics, but I didn't add that I'd run out of them), was there anything I needed?

The last question was the clincher. I did need the pills, I was almost out of milk and cornflakes, and, as she had mentioned it, could do with some orange juice and ice cream. I was at the stage when your mouth is a cesspit and your throat is coated with little shards of spiky glass. Orange juice and ice cream would go down a treat.

So I gave in and asked if she might—if it wasn't too much trouble—and if she had time—buy me the above-mentioned items and bring them for me next morning.

Reply: No trouble. Could she get in without my having to come down to open the door? Answer: How very kind, and if she came to the back door, she'd find the emergency key hidden in a tin under a flower pot, three flower pots to the left of the door.

"Not exactly a big test for an apprentice burglar," Mrs. Williamson said.

My batteries were too low to spark a laugh or a witty retort.

I'd never heard her so chirpy. But I've noticed women quite often get like that when you're under the weather and they take charge. Jane was the same. Perhaps there's something in the female genes that releases chirpiness when their maternal impulses are given full rein, not to say, reign.

And I must say, I was only too happy to be reigned. There are times when coddling is the best medicine.

Take it from me, whatever you do, do *not* volunteer to join the swelling ranks of the ancientry. Live long enough, and willy-nilly, you'll be conscripted. The benefits are limited, the perks are few and the future prospects are unattractive.

The thing to ensure is to keep your mind busy when you're young with things you can keep your mind busy with when you're old. Then, if—or rather when—your body lets you down you will still have plenty of mental pleasures to occupy you. Of course, if your mind goes before your body, who cares? You won't know anything about it.

However, there is one benefit of old age that I should mention, one cause for permanent celebration, one distinct advantage. You aren't a teenager anymore, and never will be so tediously afflicted again.

And if it's any consolation for those currently tormented by the delights of adolescence, it will soon end and there's the prospect of many years of adult pleasures ahead before being conscripted into the delights of what people these days euphemistically call "the third age," by which they mean the time of increasing decrepitude.

This is all I'm going to say on this tedious topic.

Mrs. Williamson sorted me out, fed and watered me, groomed and refreshed me with such care and attention and so efficiently that I hardly had time to grumble about it.

With me reconditioned, she started on the reason why she had phoned.

"I'm worried about Karl," she said.

Not again! I thought. Not a relapse?

"He's acting very strangely," she continued.

"Why? What's he doing?"

"That's just it. I don't know. He shuts himself up in the garden shed and is there for hours."

"Have you asked him?"

"You know what he's like. You can't get a word out of him when he doesn't want to."

"He must have said something."

"'Just messing about,' he says. 'I'll tell you later,' he says. But he's been at it all week, all the time when he's not at work."

"So he is going to work?"

"Still half-time. To be honest, I think it's time he went full-time. You know him. He has to be busy."

"You haven't looked in the shed when he's out?"

"He keeps it locked. And he blocks the window with a board when he's not there."

"How does he seem? I mean, is he depressed like before, or what?"

"No. He's better than he's been for ages. When he was

ill, he hadn't enough energy to get out of bed. Now he has more than he knows what to do with."

"From one extreme to the other."

"Exactly."

"At least he's not mooning about."

"True. Before, he was dying of breath, now he's fit to burst."

We couldn't help smiling at each other.

"Could you have a word with him?" Mrs. Williamson said. "Find out what's going on. I don't think you understand how fond he is of you and how much he listens to you."

"I don't know about that. Can't think I've said anything to him that's worth much."

"Well, I know it sounds like sucking up, saying nice things to persuade you, but it's true, whether you know it or not. Actually, I rather like it that you don't know. It's a good quality. But, anyway, would you have a try?"

I waited a moment, to be sure, before saying, "To be frank, any use or not, I'm intrigued. What on earth can he be up to?"

"So you'll have a word with him?"

Apart from being intrigued, which was a reason I was sure Mrs. Williamson would understand, I have to admit that I'd grown fond of Karl. I was concerned about him. Perhaps there was something of the paternal stirring in me after all. But there was something else as well, which I'll mention in a minute.

I said, "Phoning him won't do. He'll clam up. I'll have to see him."

Mrs. Williamson sighed with relief, but instantly looked anxious again.

"But you're not well enough," she said. "You must take care of yourself."

I was pleased she didn't add "at your age," though I suspected that's what she meant.

I was also learning she was a woman who lived on her nerves, sensitive to the smallest changes in the psychic weather. I could only imagine how much she had suffered these last months as her only child was battered and bruised, and what devastation she must have endured after the loss of her husband.

I said, "I'm feeling better already, thanks to you. I'll get up and see how I manage. If I'm OK, how about we fix for me to come to your place tomorrow? That's Saturday. Karl will be home, won't he? But we need a good excuse."

A silence for thought.

Then Mrs. Williamson perked up and said, "How about I invite you to lunch, as a thank-you for helping when Karl . . . had his episode? I think he'd like that, though he'll not admit it."

"Sounds good to me."

"All right. What about lunch tomorrow, so long as you feel up to it?"

"Thank you kindly."

"As you've been very naughty this week and not eaten

properly, it'll be best to give you something light. What about some sea bass gently poached, a few new potatoes and a salad? It's a favourite of Karl's, who'll probably do the cooking."

"Spot on! Looking forward to it already. But let me bring some ice cream for after."

"I get the impression you're an ice cream junky."

"I have to confess a slight addiction."

We both laughed, more heartily than the joke deserved, and the deal was done.

Mrs. Williamson wasn't my only visitor that day. There was another, virtual this time, not visceral. Fiorella in my inbox.

Hi, Mr. Author. I do wish you'd update yourself. Email is so yesterday. Thought I'd let you know I saw Karl today. He was with his boss doing stuff in my gran's flat. I don't know what you've all been going on about. He didn't look one bit ill. In fact, he looked in pretty good shape to me. Really, to be honest, I quite fell for him all over again. But please keep this to yourself or I'll never forgive you. I went so far as to invite him for a game of chess tomorrow but he said he was too busy. DOING WHAT? I ask you, because he wouldn't tell me. And I am consumed with curiosity. Please tell me. I'm sure you'll know. I asked him about you.

He said you'd been out for a day together. I was somewhat jealous but suppressed this unworthy reaction. Please please PLEASE tell me what he's doing. I promise not to let on to ANYONE, least of all Karl. I mean, I've just trusted you with a secret. You can trust me. I'm really really agog to know. And what do you think? Should I try and get together with him again? Do you think he wants that as well? Do you think what happened when we were away was an aberration? A one-off? Has he said anything about it? He's so lovely. I'd welcome your advice. With love from Fiorella desperado.

It was an email that switched off my reply button. Let it wait.

Had no one taught Ms. Fiorella Seabourne about appropriate register when addressing your elders, or does no one care about such niceties anymore?

But then I thought, it isn't her fault. Why do adults complain when young people do or say things badly, inappropriately, lacking manners, when it's adults who are meant to teach them how to do things properly?

So I relented.

Hi, Fiorella. I am beyond hope of updating.
Am sorry but I don't know what Karl is doing.
As for whether you should try and get together with him again, I'm afraid I am no use as an agony

uncle. And I have no idea what he wants. My own general approach to such matters is: The nose knows.

Saluté.

One more note before I finish this chapter. I mentioned earlier another reason why I wanted to know what Karl was up to.

As I've explained, I hadn't been able to write a book since Jane died. Her death seemed to kill the writer in me.

But all along, since my first meeting with Karl, in the unconscious back of my mind—the womb where all the best creative ideas have their conception and their gestation—something had been growing. And now, that Saturday, as Mrs. Williamson appealed to me, a finger reached out from my unconscious and I knew with sudden clarity the following:

The recording of Karl's encounters with me and mine with him, our shared experiences, was a story I could write.

This story would not be fiction. It would be a true-life story. I didn't have to invent anything. As yet, at that time, the end was unknown. The plot was revealing itself as we lived it.

I realised only then that it was not writing that had died when my wife died, but invention. I had had enough of invention. The facts of life, life as it is actually lived, was all that now mattered to me, all I wanted to think about, all I wanted to write about. What I had to do was set down a record of what I knew about Karl and had experienced with him. It would be his story, not my story. And that also pleased me. I had had enough of myself.

Later that day, I settled at my desk for the first time in more than a year to do what I feel I was made to do. I began making the notes, writing down all I remembered of Karl's story so far, ready to begin writing it when I knew the end.

It was, it is, in every sense, a labour of love.

EIGHTeen

- - - - - - -

YOU REMEMBER THAT EXPERIMENT WITH IRON FILINGS AND A magnet the science teacher did at school when you were of an age still easy to amaze? You remember the way the iron filings, which were scattered like a mess of dust on a sheet of paper, suddenly formed into clean strong patterns when the magnet was placed in the middle of the mess, revealing the magnet's magnetic field? Oo-arr, from the kids who'd never seen this magic before. (Do they still do that in schools?)

I was reminded of this when I arrived at the Williamsons on Saturday and saw Karl preparing lunch. Since the crisis, he had been like the mess of iron filings. Disarranged. Now he was magnetised, his filings composed into the pattern of his self. It isn't an exaggeration to say he was glowing with energy. The change was palpable. Before, he had been uneasy with himself. Now he was comfortable in his skin.

Some words from my religious past came to mind. He once was lost, and now is found.

Good spirits are infectious.

Mrs. Williamson was jocular, which I had not seen before. I caught a glimpse of what she must have been like when she was young and happily married, with infant Karl to coddle and tend.

She did a good line in joshing.

"Come and meet the master chef," she said with a wink when she let me in. And teased Karl now and then during the meal, a tickling he enjoyed while pretending poker-faced toleration of his mother's jokes.

Another pretence—that I was there as a thank-you—was kept up throughout the meal. And because nothing could be said about why I was really there, and any talk of recent unhappy events would have dampened the jollity, Mrs. Williamson plumped for the safe strategy of asking me the usual questions people ask a writer. How I got started and why, how many books I'd written and what kind. Which led by association to where I was born, and what my parents did, and what kind of boy I'd been. But no questions about my wife, for which I was grateful.

Karl listened but said nothing. He played the part of cook and waiter with the easy care I'd come to know was natural to him, whatever he did. But at the same time I sensed he'd rather I hadn't been asked about myself, and I wondered why. The clue came later.

By the time we were eating the ice cream I'd brought as my contribution, I was puzzling how to introduce the topic of Karl's activity in the shed without spooking him. I knew he'd baulk, shy away and clam up if I got it wrong. We'd finished the meal before I'd made up my mind. But need not have worried. Mrs. Williamson knew her son, and was blessed with more savvy than I'd so far guessed at.

"Have you noticed," she said to me, still in her joshing tone, "how craftsmen never clear up after themselves? They need labourers to skivvy for them. His father was like that. And like father, like son. So you two go and do whatever men do after feeding their faces, while I clear the table and wash the dishes."

She got up and began stacking the plates, and as she did so, bent over her son, kissed him on the head, and said in her genuine voice, "That was a delicious meal, my love. Thanks for making it."

"Hear, hear!" I said.

Karl affected a suitable modesty, but a blush and lowered eyes betrayed his pleasure.

"We'll help you," I said, out of politeness, but without making a move, aware of what she was up to.

"No, you won't, thank you all the same," Mrs. Williamson said. "You're a guest, and in this house guests don't do chores."

She went off into the kitchen.

I looked at Karl, smiled, and shrugged.

He got up, nodded "Follow me," and without a word

led the way through the kitchen, out the back door, down a path at the side of the lawn to a substantial shed at the bottom of the garden.

I don't mean to boast when I say I had an inkling of what I would be shown.

The shed was generously kitted out. A multitude of tools and gear neatly arranged, everything in its place. And filled with that workshop smell of sawdust and oil mixed with the tang of electricity given off by power tools. A handyman's paradise.

This was a quick impression, because my eye was caught at once by a number of objects—eight or nine—carefully placed on the workbench, like a little exhibition. They were made of thick black wire bent into a variety of shapes. Some were very simple, no more than two or three separate lengths, bent into shapes and placed together in what was clearly meant to be an intended, not an accidental, arrangement. Others were more complicated, made of one length of wire bent into elaborate, almost knotted inter-windings.

I could see the inspiration for some of them was William Tucker's sculpture, which is what I'd guessed I'd find. Others were quite different.

Words are the worst tools for describing objects. I don't know whether teachers still do it, but when I was a kid, they used to give us an exercise that began with the instruction,

"Imagine that a man from outer space has come to Earth. Describe a screwdriver to him as clearly as you can."

The spaceman, poor guy, has presumably wandered up and somehow indicated—because of course he can't speak any Earth language—that his UFO has conked out and can you help him, please. In a flash, without a moment wasted on intelligent astonishment, you give him a detailed description of a screwdriver, regardless of the fact that he cannot understand a word you're saying and assuming without further investigation that this is the implement the stranded spaceman needs.

Ah, the pleasures of school, where, we're told, we spend the happiest days of our lives!

Hard enough to describe objects with an everyday practical purpose, it's impossible to describe objects that aren't meant to be used, that don't look like anything you have seen before, and are made out of material like paint, and metal pipes, and pieces of wood and stone and clay. Sculptures. Objects made into shapes that represent nothing except the shape itself. And even if they are objects that represent things we know—landscapes, buildings, people, plants, animals, the sea, whatever—they aren't meant to be described, or presumably their makers would have used words rather than made the objects. They are objects intended for you to look at and work out what they mean from the feelings and thoughts they excite in you.

In other words, works of art.

The fact is, art objects aren't meant to be described. If

181

there's anything to be said about them it's what you want to say because of what they have done to you.

As I looked at Karl's miniature sculptures I rather dreaded he'd ask me what I thought of them and whether I liked them. I'm not good at instant reactions to anything. I need time to take in what I've experienced before I can say anything intelligent.

I'm sure most people would have asked what I thought. But Karl didn't. Another example of his difference from most people and of his sensitivity. He waited long enough for me to have a good look from various angles before he spoke.

"I know they are bad copies of the one we saw at the hotel."

I said, "Some. Not all. But I wouldn't say bad. And what does it matter if they are? Copies, I mean."

"I wanted them to be a bit different. A bit more . . . my own."

We weren't looking at each other, but at the sculptures.

I said, "When you started as a plumber, didn't your boss show you what to do and how to do it and then you did it the way he showed you?"

"Yes."

"And when your dad taught you to fish, did he show you how and then you did what he did?"

"Yes."

"Isn't that copying?"

"I suppose."

"Isn't that how we learn everything? By copying people who know how to do it and show us?"

"Hadn't thought of it like that."

There was a high stool in a corner. I sat on it. Karl hitched himself onto the workbench.

I said, "When I was fifteen, I wasn't regarded as clever, and I wasn't much of a reader. But one day I came across a book I started reading just because I had nothing else to do. I don't know why I picked it rather than another. Anyway, I started reading. It didn't hook me straightaway. It didn't have the kind of catchy opening that grabs your attention. I was well into it before this strange thing happened that had never happened before. I just couldn't stop reading it. And as I read the last page, all I wanted to do was write a book like that. I wanted it so much, I started straightaway. I still have the story. It's about eighty pages long. Eighty-one to be exact. It took me six months. When I read it now, it makes me laugh, because it's so obviously a bad copy of the book I'd read. But it got me going. It showed me what I wanted to do with my life. It showed me what *I am*."

That put a silence on both of us.

When the emotion had drained away, Karl said, "What you're saying is something like that has happened to me."

I kept my eyes, as I felt his eyes were, too, on his sculptings.

And replied, "Hasn't it?"

183

How hard it is to admit to someone else who has recognised it before you have yourself, that something has happened to you, which will reshape your life. Perhaps because you resent that they have noticed before you have. Perhaps because such an admission reveals your deepest and most vulnerable self. The self we all fear someone will injure or hurt or destroy.

And it's hard because you know at that very moment of recognition that your future is decided. That whatever happens, come what may and whether you want to or not, you will have to live your life in a way determined by your discovery of what you are and what you are meant to be.

At one and the same moment, you suddenly feel free— free to be who you are—and at the same time restricted, bound, unfree, because you can be nothing else. In gaining your freedom to be you have lost your choice of being anything else.

I sensed Karl was struggling with that very dilemma before he answered in a voice forced through a jammed mouth.

"Yes."

After such moments of a truth declared and accepted, discomfort sets in.

What should you do? Break the ice by telling a joke? Change the subject?

I thought of suggesting we leave it there for today, but that felt like dodging the questions still hanging in the air.

All I could do was take the advice I'd given Fiorella: follow my nose.

"I'm guessing these are models," I said. "D'you plan to make them the right size?"

"One or two," Karl said. "The ones I'm pleased with."

"Which are?"

He pointed to two. One very like William Tucker's, the other a more complicated arrangement of entangled and almost knotted wires.

"And making them out of pipes?"

"The Tucker one. But the other one I'd like to make out of stainless steel rods."

"And then what will you do with them?"

"I don't know. Haven't thought that far."

"You made them on the spur of the moment because you couldn't resist it?"

"I suppose . . . Yes."

Pause for thought.

"Maybe," I said, "the thing to do is make those two the size you want and then decide what to do with them?"

"Maybe . . . But is it worth it?"

So that was the question he really wanted me to answer?

I said, "Do you mean, is it worth you making them, or are they worth making?"

"Both, I guess," he said.

Pause.

"Well . . . in my opinion, yes. It's worth you making them and they are worth making."

"Why?"

Oh, please, I thought, just do it! Don't question so much!

And I was beginning to feel down. I'd forgotten the aftereffects of the 'flu during our happy meal and finding out what Karl was doing. But now started to feel queasy again.

I don't know how I'd have answered his question because before I could try there was a knock on the door.

This injected a supercharge of energy into Karl, who shot off the workbench and grabbed the door handle, while shouting, "Don't come in! Go away! Don't come in."

And Mrs. Williamson's shocked voice replying, "I won't. I've brought you some coffee."

"All right!" Karl shouted. "Put it down. I'll get it. Don't come in. Go away."

And Mrs. Williamson saying, "Yes, all right. I'm going. I'm going."

Karl waited, then opened the door enough to check his mother had gone.

Now, I'm slow to anger, which is just as well, because I'm unreasonable when roused.

And Karl's behaviour roused me.

"Just a minute!" I said, or rather heard myself explode, for anger splits you in two, or at least it does me. The angry me being angry and the normal me observing the angry me being angry.

I was beside Karl and pushing him away before I could stop myself.

"What!" Karl said.

But I paid no heed, opened the door and called after Mrs. Williamson's retreating figure, "Wait, Mrs. Williamson. Please wait!"

But she went on into the house.

I closed the door and confronted Karl and in a stern voice new to him and rare to myself said, "That was disgraceful!"

"What!"

"You should be ashamed of yourself!"

And then in a voice that matched mine, he said, "What the hell are you talking about?"

"That was your mother, for God's sake."

"I don't want her in here."

"You don't talk to your mother like that. Never! Not for any reason."

We were enraged bull to bull, close up.

"It's got nothing to do with you," he said.

"I won't stand by and say nothing when you behave so badly to your mother."

"It's none of your business."

"Have I ever interfered in your *business* before?"

No reply.

"Have I ever criticised you in any way?"

No reply.

"Have I ever told you you were wrong?"

No reply.

Karl turned away and leaned against the workbench.

I waited. Nothing.

"Have the decency to give me a reply."

"All right!" Karl said with a wave of the hand that would have pushed me away had I been in range. "All right. No."

I made myself calm down before saying, "Then give me some credit for that and listen to me now."

"I don't want her in here, that's all."

"Why not?"

"I don't want her seeing what I'm doing."

"Why not? You invited me to see it."

"That's different."

"How?"

"I thought you'd understand."

"And your mother wouldn't?"

"Yes! No! No, she wouldn't."

The anger drained from both of us. I sat down and we declined into silence.

Now I was upset with myself for losing my temper.

They say you should never apologise and never explain, because it shows a sign of weakness.

Baloney.

That's the cause of vendettas, endless cycles of revenge and the interminable abomination of war.

And I know something else. It's the older, and the stranger, who must break the circle.

I forced myself to say, "I'm sorry. I lost my temper."

Karl said nothing. Nor did I want him to. Mutual

apologies don't heal the wound, they only put a bandage over it.

I said, "Do something for me."

Karl remained silent.

"Let me ask your mother to join us. Show her what you've done and see what she says."

No reply.

"Put yourself in her shoes, Karl. You're her only son. Her only child. She adores you. Quite literally, she'd die for you. I think you know that. She's gone through a hell of worry about you these last few months. Now she sees her beloved son full of life again. And it's obvious whatever has happened has something to do with what you're doing in here. Don't you think you ought to show her? Even if she doesn't understand. Isn't it the right thing to do?"

Still he remained silent, but took a deep, deep breath and let it out as if he were expelling poisoned air.

A few moments passed again before I said, "Shall I go and get her?"

He nodded.

When she was upset, Jane used to talk about "crying inside." I thought of that when I found Mrs. Williamson sitting at the kitchen table, no longer chirpy, no longer the happy woman she had been during our meal, and everything about her betraying how hurt she felt. There were no tears in her eyes, but I was sure she was crying inside.

I sat down at the table, opposite her.

I said, "Karl wants you to join us in the shed."

She said, head down and with an effort, "I hoped we were through with this."

I said, "I think you are."

She let out a heavy sigh.

"Then why . . ."

"I think this is different."

She looked at me, a hard angry look I hadn't seen from her before.

"Different?" she said. "What's different about it?"

"He was rude. I know. But I don't think he meant to be. I don't think he meant to hurt you. Or reject you."

"That's certainly how it felt."

"Yes."

"Well, then?"

"I can only tell you how it seems to me. I'm not saying I'm right."

She didn't respond. For the first time I wondered whether Karl's reticence, whether his refusal to speak when he was upset or facing a difficulty in himself, came from his mother, and not, as I'd assumed, from his father. Maybe he wasn't so much his father's child as his mother's boy?

I said, "This didn't happen because he's depressed again. It happened because he isn't ready to show you what he's doing in the shed."

"He showed you. Why not me? Do I mean so much less to him?"

"No! Just the opposite."

She gave a huffy laugh.

"He showed it to me because I don't mean to him what you do."

"Well, I'm glad you understand it, because I certainly don't."

I waited a moment to let the sparks die.

Then I said, "When I was starting out as a writer, I hated showing anyone what I was writing before I'd finished it. I feared that if they said it was no good, I'd feel so crushed I'd give up. Especially if it was my parents who didn't like it. Even when I finished it I didn't want my parents to read it. Not till someone else had said it was OK. Someone whose opinion my parents respected."

Mrs. Williamson gave me a searching look.

"Is he writing something then?"

"No."

"So what is he doing?"

"I think that's for him to tell you."

"And he's sent you to fetch me?"

"Yes."

"Why couldn't he come for me himself?"

"It's too hard for him."

"He didn't have any difficulty telling me to go away."

By now I knew she was being deliberately stubborn. Of course she understood! She was an intelligent woman. She knew her son. She'd been through worse than this with him. I was pretty sure this wasn't the first time he'd been rude to her. I knew what it was like when you were in the pit of depression. You want the person closest to you to attend, but at the same time you want to be left alone. An emotional double bind. And you are hurting so much you can't help passing the hurt on.

Mrs. Williamson knew this. But Karl seemed to be out of the pit now, and she had been shocked by his behaviour because she feared it meant he'd reverted. What's more, there was hurt from those bad months locked up inside her, where she'd kept it while Karl was ill so as not to make things worse, and to show him that nothing he did, however bad, would turn her away from him or cause her to treat him as badly as he had treated her. She thought this was over, but his sudden rudeness had churned the pent-up bile, which she couldn't help letting out a bit on me.

As for Karl, now that he was his best self again and something was happening to him he only half understood— something bright and new he didn't yet know how to deal with—he was protecting himself in case this bright new thing was taken from him before he'd grasped it.

And me? I was an outsider, sympathetic to both mother and son. And quite often an outsider can see what's going on between two people when the two people are blind to it.

There was something else I thought I understood, but didn't mention to Mrs. Williamson.

Karl is an only son and I'm an only son. I've known others during my life. And have observed that they—we— tend to behave in one of two ways with our mothers. Some are deeply attached, tell their mother everything, and do nothing without discussing it with her. Others keep their distance, are reserved, tell their mothers as little as possible about what they are doing. I was of the second kind. And by now I knew Karl was too.

But unless you're intent on deliberately hurting your mother, which I never was and I believed Karl wasn't, there are some important things in your life you have to reveal. And just as I had to tell my mother I was trying to be a writer because of how hurt I knew she would be if I didn't, so I knew it was necessary for Karl to explain to his mother what he was trying to do that made him closet himself secretively in the shed. I was sure he had to do this because I had left revealing what I was up to till it was too late. The breach this caused between myself and my mother was never repaired. I didn't want that to happen to Karl.

I knew if it went wrong, neither of them would have anything more to do with me.

"Will you go and see?" I asked.

She smiled and said, "Course I will! Did you think for one second that I wouldn't?"

I laughed.

We were friends again.

She got up.

I was going to, but suddenly felt quite done in.

Mrs. Williamson waited. "Are you all right? You don't look so good."

"The bloody 'flu," I said. "Overdone it a bit, first day out. Enjoyed myself too much."

"Have a lie down on the sofa in the sitting room."

"Kind of you. But, if you don't mind, I think I'll just slope off home and go to bed."

"You sure? Shall I get Karl to drive you?"

"No, no. You go and see him. Very important. I'll manage. Really. Say good-bye to him for me, and tell him I'm sorry to duck out but I'll be in touch."

"Of course! And you're sure you'll be OK?"

"I will. Honestly."

As soon as I got home, I went to bed and was a goner for the next five hours. When I woke, I felt like I'd been squashed by an avalanche.

NINETEEN

NEXT DAY, A SUNDAY, I MADE A BET WITH MYSELF THAT MRS.
Williamson would phone to ask how I was.

By the way, how do you make a bet with yourself? With
whom are you betting? This brings me back to that endlessly
puzzling, endlessly fascinating question: When I'm talking
to myself, whom am I talking to and who is doing the
talking? Are we all in fact two people, not one? Are we all
One and Another? What I know is that I have an "everyday
self," the one who does things, says things, deals with the
ins and outs, ups and downs of daily life, and another, an
"inner self," the one I think of as my real self, the self who
observes everything my everyday self does, comments and
judges, praises and dispraises, considers what would be best
to do and not to do, and assesses the results.

Whichever one of me bet Mrs. W. would phone is the
one who won. (But won what?)

Typical of her thoughtfulness, she waited till late morning, in case, as she said, I wanted to sleep in.

We exchanged the usual routine conversational strokes: How was I this morning? Much better, thank you. And her? Very well, thank you. Had I recovered from yesterday? Yes, and how much I'd enjoyed our meal. And how much she had too.

Those pleasantries out of the way, I asked whether she had gone to see Karl in the shed.

Yes, she had.

What did she make of what she saw?

She'd been so surprised, she didn't know what to think.

So what had she said?

Nothing. She didn't have to. As soon as she'd looked at the things on the workbench, Karl told her they were little models.

"I said, 'Models of what?' He said they were models of sculptures he was thinking of making full sized. I asked him where he got the idea from. He said he'd seen some sculptures when he went with you the other day, and he just felt he wanted to make something like them. So he was trying out some ideas with bits of wire because it would be too expensive to experiment with metal tubes and rods."

"And what did you say?"

"I asked him why he hadn't wanted me to know what he was doing. He said he didn't want to show me till he was sure it wasn't a passing fad. So I asked why he'd

shown them to you. He said you'd understand what he
was trying to do, and it wouldn't matter so much if he
gave up after that. I asked him why he'd decided to show
me now. Did that mean he'd go on? He said you'd told
him it was wrong to show you and not to show me. He
said he hadn't meant to hurt me, but if I'd not liked
what he was doing it would upset him and put him off.
I said I understood now why he hadn't told me. I was
glad he was doing something that made him happy and
I hoped he'd go on with it, and I'd help him any way
I could. We gave each other a hug and that was that. I
went back into the house and Karl went on working in
the shed."

I said, "So you didn't talk about the models?"

"No," Mrs. W. said. "Which was just as well, because I
wouldn't have known what to say. They just looked like bits
of bent wire to me."

I said, "That's all they are, in a way."

Mrs. W. laughed and said, "I'm sure he thinks they're
more than that, but what? Do you know?"

"I'm not sure yet."

"He didn't tell you?"

"No. I guess they represent ideas. Feelings. Thoughts."

"You mean abstract art?"

"If you want to call it that."

"I'm not too good with abstract art. I like art that looks
like things I know."

"Maybe most people do."

"And you?"

"I like some and not all. I think some of it is a load of old tosh. Pretentious nonsense. Some of it is wonderful. But that's true of everything, isn't it?"

Pause.

Mrs. W. said, "D'you think he wants to be a sculptor? I mean professionally?"

"I've no idea."

"He hasn't said?"

"And I haven't asked."

"But if he does, won't he have to go to art school, to learn how to do it properly?"

"Not necessarily. He could find a job as an assistant to a sculptor and learn that way."

"You mean, like an apprenticeship? Like he learned his plumbing?"

"Why not? That's the way it used to be done for centuries, till we all got hung up on going to college and getting bits of paper to prove we're supposed to be able to do something we learn best by doing it."

"But isn't it hard to make a living as a sculptor?"

"Harder than making a living as a plumber, that's for sure."

"Oh dear!"

Pause.

"Will you encourage him, if he decides to do it as a job?" Mrs. W. said, her voice giving away her worry.

"You'd rather I didn't?"

"Wouldn't he be better off as a plumber and doing his sculpting as a hobby?"

"Well, let's see how things develop."

"But you'll not push him into it?"

"No, I'll not push him into anything."

Pause.

"There's something else," Mrs. W. said.

"What's that?"

"He had another visitor yesterday, not long after you'd gone."

"Oh?"

"Fiorella."

"*Fiorella!* What did she want?"

"To see Karl of course."

"And?"

"I made her wait while I asked him. He told me to send her to the shed."

"And?"

"And nothing! Karl came in about an hour later. I asked him where Fiorella was. He said she left by the back gate. I asked what she wanted. He said, just to see him. I asked if he'd shown her his models. He said he had."

"And that was it?"

"That was it. You know my Karl well enough by now. If he doesn't want to tell you something, wild horses won't drag it out of him."

"Well, that's a turnup for the book!"

This bolt of news rather knocked me off balance. What was Fiorella up to? And what was Karl up to, allowing her to see his models? And what else went on between them? And why had she chosen that day to drop in on him uninvited? Or was she uninvited? Had something gone on between them which Karl preferred I didn't know about? I felt pretty sure he'd have mentioned it, had he and Fiorella got together again. Or would he?

To be truthful, I felt miffed that he might be keeping something like this from me. But I knew, at the same time, there was no reason why he should confide in me—about this or anything else. And I had to confess to myself that feeling miffed was a sign that I was assuming too much, expecting too much, of our friendship, and that I was more concerned about him, and wanted to be closer to him, than I should allow myself to want.

The only thing I could think to say was, "Where is he now?"

But the way I said it gave away my too-keen interest.

"Gone fishing," Mrs. W. said.

I thought it best not to go any further. And she must have thought so too, because she added,

"Is there anything you need? Anything I can bring for you?"

I said, no, thanks, I was OK.

Pause.

"You can call me anytime," she said.

I knew she meant to reassure me.

We went though the usual chatter before ringing off.

I thought that would be it for the rest of the day and settled down to read the Sunday papers. But no.

TWENTY

As you know *everything* about Karl, you are bound to know what he is doing with bits of wire. I went to see him yesterday. I know I said I wouldn't. I know he doesn't like surprises. (I think he is probably a control freak.) But I couldn't help myself, I was desperate to see him, I wish I wasn't but I was, I mean I still am. I thought he wouldn't see me but he did. He was in the garden shed. I wouldn't say he was exactly ecstatic. Very arm's-length and hands-off, when what I wanted was close-up and intimate and hands-on. As a matter of fact, most of the time I was there I felt I was being watched, being *observed*, like I was some kind of laboratory specimen. Also like I was being *tested* and *assessed*

202

and *examined*. I tried to be cool and offhand and all that but when I'm unsure of myself I start to babble, yammer yammer yammer. I do wish I didn't do this. It is so *gauche*. I know I'm doing it at the time and keep telling myself to *shut up*, but can't stop myself, can't help it, it really is a pain. So I went on blathering at him, it doesn't matter what I said, about nothing really. And he just stood there listening and watching and *saying nothing*. Until after *an age* he asked me why I'd come—I said because I wanted to see him, no other reason— and he asked how I was getting on—school, chess, blah blah. I asked about him but he did that trick of answering my questions with questions about me. And instead of pushing him to talk about himself I stupidly rabbitted on again about myself. I think I do this, with him anyway, because what I really want to do is get hold of him and etc. etc. There's just something about him that makes me want to do that, there's something small boy and vulnerable about him and at the same time something terribly grown-up and strong and I have to admit I find that combination plus his looks, his body, etc., irresistible. I guess blathering on is a kind of compensation or something for not being allowed to touch him and hold him. I suppose I'm trying to touch him and hold him and kiss him with words.

Now I'm rabbitting on to you and not getting to the point. Why am I doing that? It's important to know why you do what you do, especially the things you do without meaning to, don't you agree? I know you agree because all your books are like that, which is one reason why I like them. So why am I rabbitting on to you now? (Pause for thought.) Oh dear, I don't like what I'm thinking. (Pause for more thought.) Well, alright, what it is, I think, is—I don't know how to put it without sounding stupid or bitchy—but I half resent you knowing Karl better than I do and seeing him all the time and I don't, and half resent Karl knowing you and seeing you, because after all he only got to know you because of me talking to him about your books (which he hasn't read, by the way, I know because I asked him yesterday, but then, you know he doesn't read novels or anything he doesn't have to, but only what he really wants to, and why he doesn't). Does this mean I'm jealous? I hope it doesn't. I hate the thought that I might be a jealous person. It's such an ugly weakness. And am I being like some silly girl who comes wittering on because she thinks she's been left out of the game and wants to worm her way in and be best friends with the other two and goes smarming up to them trying to ingratiate herself? God, I hope not!

The only way to stop wittering like this is to stop wittering. So:

LONG PAUSE FOR RECOVERY OF CALM.

Much later.

Here is my point in best exam-essay style:

I had not been in Karl's shed, which he called his workshop, before, so everything in it was new to me. To stop myself blathering on I asked about the use of some of the tools and machines. Karl replied briefly. There were some bits of wire on the workbench, which I didn't take any notice of, because I thought they were bits of rubbish. All the time, Karl was standing at the end of the bench, leaning back against it.

Having looked round the shed (sorry, workshop), and hoping he would allow me to get close now that we had gone round the houses with reconnecting chatter, I ended my tour beside him, intending to lean against the bench in the same posture as him. But as I did this he said with alarm, Hey! Careful! and put his hand on my back to stop me leaning against the bench.

My instant thought was that he did this because he didn't want me so close to him. But in the next instant I realised he was keeping me from maybe disturbing the bits of wire.

Karl didn't say anything, just kept looking at me with that observer's eye. I felt he was waiting for me to say something special, something important, but I couldn't think what it was. Again, I felt I was being tested.

Of course I understood from what he'd done that these bits of wire weren't just bits of rubbish.

Thinking it would please him if I showed some interest, I reached out to pick one up, but he caught me by the wrist and said, Don't touch! (Come to think of it, this could be taken as the motto for the day.)

I said I was sorry and asked if they were something special. He said they were. I asked why. He said they were little models. I asked what of. He said, What do you think? I said I had no idea. And instantly felt a dreadful failure, which made me want to run away, but I was determined not to let him get the better of me. Which is another thing about him. He is very powerful.

Anyway and anyhow I said I didn't know and Karl said, Guess.

Well, I thought, I'm not going to play this game, I've had enough of it.

I said, You're being horrible to me.

He said, No, I'm not.

I said, Yes, you are. I came to see you, to find out how you are, because I know you haven't been too great lately, and you're treating me like I'm something the cat dragged in, like a *child*, and like you're some kind of teacher condescending to a stupid pupil. You are *patronising me* and I don't like it!

Have a guess, he said, as if I hadn't uttered a word.

That really did me in!

I said, sharp as I could, I have no idea what you mean or what these nasty-looking bits of wire are for. And to be honest, Karl, I don't care.

He smiled then. The observer look vanished. He scratched his head. And then said, all politeness and public good manners, Sorry if I upset you. Good of you to call. I'm OK. Doing well, thanks.

Which meant, clear as day, the visit was over. He didn't exactly go to the door and open it, but he might as well have done.

I said, See you around, and left by the back gate to avoid Mrs. Williamson and her questions.

So, Mr. Writer. What's going on? What is so special about those bits of wire?

Please tell me.

I *have* to know.

Your reader, Fiorella

These days, everyone expects instant replies—to emails, texts, blogs, tweets, and who knows what else has been added to the techno list before you read this sentence? I knew Fiorella would be checking her inbox every few minutes. But decided not to submit to the universal imperative for the instantaneous. She could wait, while I decided what to say to her. If anything.

And it's just as well I did.

TWEnTY-OnE

- - - - - - -

FOUR O'CLOCK. SIXTEEN HUNDRED HOURS. THE FRONT DOORBELL.
Dusk falling. No callers without appointment. No one had
an appointment.

I spied from my workroom window. The top of Karl's
head in view.

When I opened the door, he was holding out to his
sides, cruciform, one in each hand, a couple of trout, his
face alive with a broad grin.

"Your supper," he said. "I'll cook it, if you like."

He put the fish in the kitchen sink, asked to use the
bathroom, returned, washed and brushed up and burnished
from a day in river air, his outdoor gear removed, back in
his regulation uniform of black crewneck sweater and jeans.
He set to work cleaning and gutting the fish, preparing
potatoes and salad.

I sat at the kitchen table and watched.

"How are you feeling?" he asked.

"Fine. And to what do I owe the honour of this visit?"

"I brought you the fish," he said, scrubbing away, but he wasn't a good liar. There was a giveaway wobble in his voice.

"I can tell there's something. So stop fussing with the fish and come clean."

A tense moment. I could feel him holding himself down. Then he swilled his hands under the tap and dried them on a towel. He turned to me, but didn't look at me. "I want to know," came out in a burst, "what you think."

Typical Karl! Fill in the gaps. He was an expert at indeterminacy.

"About your models and making sculptures?"

He nodded, still no eye contact.

I said, "I've thought a lot about that since yesterday."

"And?"

"I'm glad you've come. There's something I want to show you. And then I have a couple of questions."

I led him out into the front garden, where I sat on the sitting room windowsill and indicated to him to sit beside me. There was just enough daylight left.

"Look at the garden," I said. "What do you see?"

"What d'you mean?"

"What I say. What do you see?"

He looked. Shook his head.

"Well. The garden. The lawn. A border of lavender along the path. The wall with the road on the other side . . . I dunno! . . . What am I supposed to see?"

I walked to the centre of the lawn. And stooped over, one arm bent over my neck, the other arm stuck straight up at an angle, and peered at him from under that arm.

It wasn't an easy pose to hold. But I managed to stay there long enough for the brow-wrinkled puzzlement on Karl's face to be wiped clean by the dawn of perception.

And then, both of us realising the ridiculousness of my contorted pose, we spluttered into laughter.

I uncurled myself and returned to the windowsill.

I said, "I'll pay for the materials."

An unhurried pause.

Before Karl said, "I don't know what to say."

I said, "I'd say, yes, thank you, if I were you."

"But what if you don't like it?"

"You'll make a model first?"

"I'd need to."

"Then we can go step by step."

"It's a good place."

"If it's the right size. And shape as well, of course."

"Would fit the garden. And be good against the view of the valley."

"And I could look down at it from my workroom, which would give another angle."

"And another from the bottom of the garden and the road, looking towards the house."

"So what do you say?"

I felt rather than heard his chuckle.

He thought some more.

Then, parodying me, "Yes, thank you."

"Done!" I said. "Let's go back inside. I shall get piles, if I sit on this cold ledge much longer."

As we went in, I suggested he get on with the cooking while we talked.

I sat at the table, and said, "There's a few things I'd like to ask you."

"Go ahead."

"Are you thinking of becoming a professional sculptor?"

"And nothing else?"

"Yes."

"No."

"So it's a hobby?"

"No."

"Explain."

"I do want to make sculptures. I've been doing a lot of looking on the internet. I'm getting an idea of what's possible. And I do want to show them. Like the ones we saw at the hotel. In natural places, not art galleries. And I'll sell them if anybody wants them, which I doubt."

"You haven't made any yet, so you can't know."

"Yeah, but."

"That sounds like being a professional to me."

"But I want to keep on being a plumber."

"OK. I can see you need to make a living. But if you make it as a sculptor?"

"I don't know if I can explain this very well. I've only

thought of it these last few days. And I haven't talked to anybody about it."

"Is this why you came to see me today?"

"Yes."

"I'm privileged."

"Yeah, yeah!"

"I mean it. So try me."

"Well . . . Sculpture is, like, an art, isn't it?"

"It's an art, yes."

"I don't know anything about art. I've never thought much about it. But what I think is art is kind of personal, if you know what I mean? Artists do it to please themselves, don't they?"

"You can put it like that. I'd say the best artists, and the great artists, do it because they have to."

"You mean, they can't help it?"

"They don't feel they have any choice about it."

"I don't quite get what you mean."

"Let's see . . . You had a choice about becoming a plumber. You could have been an electrician or a carpenter or anything like that. Yes?"

"Yes."

"What I'm trying to say is some people do things because they feel they have to. Some people paint pictures or make sculptures because they want to. They choose to do it. But some people do it because they feel that's what they *must* do."

"You mean, like it's their fate?"

"I'm not keen on thinking of it as fate, but it'll do for now."

"But still . . . What are they doing . . . with it?"

"They aren't doing anything *with it*. They're just making something. Making an object."

"Like you tried to explain to me the other day?"

"That's it."

"But why?"

"Why did you make those models? Why do you want to make them into sculptures?"

He finished what he was doing and sat down.

"I don't know!"

There was desperation in his voice.

"Do you need to know?"

"Yes!"

"Tell me if I'm wrong, but I'm guessing you feel you can't help doing it."

"Sort of. Yes."

"Isn't it enough to know you can't help it?"

"No!"

"Maybe you can't know why you have to do it until you've done it. And done it more than once or twice but many times. Maybe it's by doing it you find out why you're doing it."

"But you must have some idea why real artists do it."

"I think there are probably a number of reasons."

"All right. Give me one."

I didn't want to. I didn't want him to think the reason I gave was the best or the only worthy reason.

"Come on," he said, almost violently. "Tell me!"

"All right, all right! . . . I think the main reason is that it's the only way they know how to make sense of themselves and the only way they can make sense of life. It's the only way they know how to say something about themselves and about life they feel they *need* to say."

He looked at me with the kind of hard stare that's unnerving. Fiorella was right. He had a power that could floor you. It was like there was a generator inside that had been running at low power all the time I'd known him and had now revved up to full capacity.

"Is that how it is for you?" he said.

I didn't want to answer.

"*Is it?*"

I nodded.

He said, sharp as acid, "Strikes me you're saying you do it to keep yourself alive."

That put a stop on me. It had taken me years as a writer before I understood this about myself, yet Karl was saying it as if it was simple and obvious.

He got up and went on with the cooking.

After a few minutes he said, "I don't want to do something that's only for myself all the time. I want to do something else as well. Something that's ordinary and practical and useful to other people. I want to make sculptures, but I want to go on plumbing too."

"You don't think sculpture is practical and useful?"

"Not the same way plumbing is. People really need

plumbers, don't they? It's not much good having sculptures if your house is flooding or you've got no water, is it?"

I'd had enough philosophising about art for one night so I didn't take up the challenge. Let him think it out for himself.

He turned to me with his fish slice in his hand like a weapon.

"Well, is it?"

"I take your point."

"I want to do both. If you're talking about what I *need* to do, I need to do both."

"Even if you were a successful sculptor you'd still want to be a plumber?"

"Yes, that's what I'm saying, OK?"

"I'm not trying to dissuade you. In fact, I think it's admirable."

He turned back to his cooking. "You do?"

"I do. I think I understand what you mean. I think what you're saying is that going on with plumbing isn't about making a living, though it will do that. It's about you not losing touch with everyday life and ordinary people."

"And because I think I'll be a better sculptor the better I am as a plumber."

"And vice versa?"

"That as well."

Enough! We'd said enough. Say more and we'd kill it. To make a break I did something I hadn't done since I was a boy. I drink wine and don't like beer. Karl preferred beer. I have an old jug that belonged to my grandfather, my father's father. Before dinner he used to fill the jug with beer from his own little barrel (a firkin he kept in the dining room). When my father, who told me about this, was big enough to hold the jug when it was full, my grandfather let him do it. After he told me this story, my dad let me do it once, by taking the jug to the local pub, filling it and bringing it back for my father. Just so I'd done it too.

Now I took the jug, which I've always treasured and never used in case it was broken, went to the pub up the road, and brought it back full of beer for Karl.

I was halfway home when I remembered that I'd said something to Karl's mother during his crisis about how writing helped me to survive. Maybe Mrs. W. had told him this. Maybe he wasn't so clever after all. Maybe he was only repeating what his mother had told him I'd said.

But then I thought, So what? Which of us ever has an original thought, however clever we are? I haven't. Everything I say that's worth saying I've come across somewhere else—have heard it or read it. Why should I think any the less of Karl for doing the same? At least he'd remembered and said it on an appropriate occasion. That's clever enough. Or maybe, maybe after all, he hadn't been told it by his mother and really had thought it for himself.

I served Karl some of the beer, gratified by his pleasure at what I'd done. And while he finished cooking, I excused myself—extending the break and the silence—went to my workroom and fiddled with some papers, shelved a few stray books, returning to the kitchen when Karl shouted up the stairs that our meal was ready.

By unspoken mutual agreement we said no more then about art or his plans.

I was tempted to ask him about Fiorella. I was dying to know why he had treated her the way she described and to hear his side of the story. I hoped he might bring it up. But he didn't and I couldn't find a way of mentioning her without him wondering why and it being obvious she had been in touch.

So the evening ended with questions secluded in the air.

TWENTY-TWO

- - - - - - -

THAT NIGHT, BEFORE SHUTTING DOWN THE COMPUTER ON THE way to bed, I checked my emails.

Another from Fiorella:

Did you receive my email this afternoon? In case you didn't, here it is again.

On the spur of the moment and without giving it a second thought, I clicked Reply and wrote:

Think artefact.

If she was as keen a reader of my books as she said she was, she wouldn't have much trouble working out what I meant.

TWENTY-THREE

- - - - - - -

FOR THE NEXT THREE WEEKS I HEARD NOTHING FROM KARL.

Mrs. W. phoned every two or three days to ask after me, and keep me up to date. Karl was plumbing full-time now, eating "like there was no tomorrow," sleeping "like a baby." A complete change from the bad times. He spent his evenings in his workshop. He said nothing about what he was doing. On Sundays he went fishing. But he wasn't seeing friends or anyone and she was worried in case he became reclusive and too self-absorbed. As someone who prefers to be on my own I had nothing to offer by way of advice or sympathy.

Fiorella hadn't shown up again. Karl hadn't mentioned her. But that didn't mean they hadn't been in touch by what Mrs. W. called "virtual chat."

Late in the morning of the fourth Sunday after our fish

supper, Karl phoned. Could he come over and show me something?

He arrived on his bike at two. He had his backpack. When he came inside, he took out a cardboard box, which he set down on the kitchen table and out of which he took what I knew at once was the model of the sculpture for my front garden.

Attached to the base was a little paper plaque on which was written "Fishing for Words."

I could see what he intended. Wires that would be metal rods rose up from various irregular points round the circular base. The wires were shaped like lines cast from fishing rods, curving up into the air at irregular heights, some caught in mid-flight and some turning down into the base. By their overlapping they formed a kind of net. Inside the base was a bowl, which, as I looked, Karl filled with water. Then I saw how the ends of some of the lines dipped into the water.

"It's only to give you an idea," Karl said. "I'll make the lines of different metals, like black rods and stainless steel and copper so they catch the light differently. That'll give it some colour. And I'm going to cut letters out of a sheet of metal, and I'll burnish them to give them different tones as well, and scatter them in the bottom of the pool. And you see? The pool will be a birdbath. I thought of including a fountain coming up from the middle that would burst over the top of the lines so that there was a spray of lines of water as well, and that would make everything shine wet in the sunlight. I could plumb in the water supply."

I said, "It's brilliant!" And I meant it.

The model was only a hint. But I could imagine the finished thing and was touched and excited by the way he'd combined his love of fishing with my love of words, and the idea of writing being like fishing, and how he'd given the sculpture a practical use that included natural life. In a way, the thing was like a birdcage without being a cage. He'd planned the way the lines crossed and crisscrossed to leave plenty of spaces for smaller birds to get in and out without feeling trapped.

I said, "A lot will depend how big the real one is, and the proportions, don't you think?"

"I wondered if we could work out how big it should be?"

We talked this over and ended up in the front garden with a couple of kitchen chairs, arranging them on top of each other and on their sides and upside down and all such combinations, measuring the results with a tape measure, trying to work out the best dimensions. Finally, we got some sticks of bamboo I used for runner beans and did what we could to mock up a grid the height and footprint we thought would be about right for the sculpture.

We were at it for over an hour. But at last felt we had cracked it. We'd agreed the precise spot on the lawn, the height and diameter, the area and depth of the birdbath and how to construct it. And came back inside after clearing up, feeling cold from the chill of the winter evening but sparkling with excitement.

In all our times together so far, this was the first time I felt we were enjoying ourselves, without strain or any sense of difference of age or of deference, concession or inequality. It was, I thought afterwards, the first time we had met as ourselves, untrammelled, unguarded and in tune.

I was glad Karl set off for home as soon as we finished planning. To have gone on would have risked blemish.

TWENTY-FOUR

THE IDEA FOR THE PARTY WAS MRS. WILLIAMSON'S. SHE SAID it was to celebrate the installation of Karl's first sculpture. I'm sure she meant it, but I'm also sure she used it as an excuse to bring together with Karl some of the friends he'd neglected since the onset of his crisis six months ago.

His pals from the rugby club came, and his boss from work, Mr. Cooksley, and, I was surprised to find, Fiorella, who brought her friend Becky, no doubt for moral support, though it crossed my mind that the typical combination of pretty (Fiorella) and plain (Becky) was meant to work to Fiorella's advantage.

When Mrs. W. first mooted it, I wasn't keen. My energy sank to zero at the prospect of the preparations as well as the party itself. But in order to please her, I agreed, assuming that Karl in his present mood wouldn't. When she told me he had, I swore to myself and asked how she'd done it. To which I received an enigmatic "mothers have their ways."

I didn't find out till the day of the party what her mother's way was. A midday event so that there'd be enough daylight for inspection of the installation before the winter evening set in. Mrs. W. was titivating the food and drink in the kitchen. I was hovering with Karl in the sitting room. Karl was upset because he hadn't had time to fix the sculpture permanently. The rods were still loose, supporting each other just enough to keep them in place. ("And hope to heaven there isn't a strong puff of wind or the whole shebang will collapse," Karl said.) He planned to come back the next day to fix it permanently.

To add to the stress and strain, we were both suffering those awkward moments before a party when everything is ready and you're waiting for the guests to arrive, wondering if any will turn up and how you'll get through it, when Karl said, "Why did you let her do this?"

"Me?" I said. "It's not my fault! Why did you?"

"I thought you'd say no."

"And I thought you would."

"What? You said yes because you thought I'd say no?"

"And you said yes because you thought I'd say no?"

Pause for computation of one and one.

"When did she ask you?" Karl said.

I told him.

"That was before she asked me."

225

"And she didn't tell you I'd said yes?"

"No, she didn't."

"And if she had?"

"I'd have said no way!"

"Well, I'll be jiggered!"

Karl grinned at me. "You still haven't cottoned on to my mother, have you?"

"What d'you mean?"

"You think she's as nice as pie, straight as a die, and wouldn't say boo to a goose."

"Do I?"

"But it's a front. My dad used to say she was more canny than a con man and trickier than a conjuror. As innocent as a dove, he said, and as cunning as a serpent."

"Are you saying she's unscrupulous?"

"Wouldn't go as far as that. She's clever at getting what she wants. But she does have her limits."

"Does she?"

"She knows how to twist you round her little finger, that's for sure. Plays the fading flower and you fall for it."

"Me naïve? I'm shocked!"

"You fall for it because you want to. I can tell by the way you look at her."

"So this is a day for telling truths."

"She's just as bad about you. I'd go for it, if I was you."

"Don't be so ridiculous."

"I wouldn't mind, if that's what's holding you back."

"Nothing is holding me back. But even if you're right,

which you're not, think of your mother's age and mine. She could be my daughter."

"What's that got to do with it?"

"More than you can yet know, young man."

"Yes, Granddad."

Luckily at that moment the first guests arrived. A scrummage of Karl's rugger pals.

So we had a party.

To adapt a well-known quotation: All happy parties are the same, each unhappy party is unhappy in its own way.

At the time, this seemed to me to be a happy party. As I am not making things up and it is not a novel but an account of events in real life, all I can say is that during the party everyone seemed to me to behave well, so far as behaving well at parties goes. Karl's sculpture was admired, though not without some teasing by his rugger pals, and the guests departed without overstaying their welcome and before the food and drink ran out.

That said, there was one incident that might have marred the proceedings. We were all out in the garden viewing the sculpture. Mrs. W. insisted, much to Karl's discomfit, that we "raise a glass to Karl's work." We did as instructed. At that moment a gang of young men were sloping by on the road, tins of beer in their hands, and well oiled with booze. I recognised them at once: the same four who sat next to us in the pub and riled Karl the night of the fracas. They saw us, stopped, jeered, blew raspberries, and indicated by various gestures what we should do with ourselves.

Karl bridled at this. As did his rugger pals. War would undoubtedly have been declared were it not for the intervention of Karl's boss, Mr. Cooksley, who announced in the stentorian tones of a sergeant major on the parade ground, which outclassed the baying of the yobs by a good margin of decibels, "Steady, the Buffs!"*

I doubt very much that Karl or his pals had heard this ancient command before. But the manner of its delivery carried such authority and its meaning was so plain that it had the effect of restraining Karl and his pals and, more astonishingly, silencing the yobs, who wandered on their inebriated way with a few yeowls and whoops to save face.

---

* Karl and his pals might not have heard this before, but I had. It was common in my childhood as a warning not to take any impulsive action you might regret or would be inappropriate at the time. I didn't know then, though I do now, that it originated in 1858 on the island of Malta, where the 2nd Battalion, the Royal East Kent Regiment, was stationed. The regiment was one of oldest in the British Army, dating back to 1572. They were called "the Buffs" because at one time their uniforms were made of light brown leather. In 1858 they were quartered with the Royal North British Fusiliers, with whom there was some rivalry. One day on the parade ground, this rivalry would have led to competitive unseemliness, but it was forestalled by the very strict Royal Kent adjutant, a Scot named Cotter, who brooked no disobedience. He called out, "Steady, the Buffs!" and the brewing trouble was dispelled. From that day the Royal Kents used this as their battle cry, until in 1961 the regiment was amalgamated with others and is today part of the Princess of Wales Royal Regiment. I offer this item of useless information for your edification and amusement.

After which, with huffs and smiles and raised eyebrows from the older of us, and some rumbling irritation among the younger, the party continued with pretended disregard of the interruption.

Later, when I tackled him about it, I gathered from Mr. Cooksley that he'd spent eleven years in the army, where he reached the rank of warrant officer, which explained his expert and timely intervention.

We were looking at Karl's sculpture.

"What d'you think?" I asked him.

"Not my cup of tea, to be honest," he said.

"You don't like it?"

"It's well made. But so it should be!" He smiled. "I taught him."

"But you're not too keen?"

"I don't see what he's trying to do. I like pictures, sculptures, that sort of thing, to look like they are meant to be."

"He means it to be what he feels. About fishing. What fishing feels like. What it means to him."

"Well, it's beyond me. But I'll tell you this. I'm pleased he wants to do it. His dad would have been pleased as well."

"You knew his dad."

"He was my best friend. Grew up together. Same schools. He was brainier than me. Went off and did engineering at college, built up his business. But never forgot where he came from. Never any airs and graces. And never forgot his old friends."

"You must miss him."

"You could say."

"And Karl. You must have known him since he was born."

"I was with his dad in the maternity ward the night he arrived."

"So, since his father died, you must have been like a second father to him."

Mr. Cooksley gave a huffing smile. "No, no! Nobody could replace him. I've never seen a father and son so close. Did everything together from day one. Too close. I used to think it wasn't good for a lad to be that attached. And I was right. The loss of his dad devastated him."

"But you've been a big help."

"Done what I could. For him and his mother. She and my wife are as good friends as his dad and I were. Boyhood sweethearts we both married. Not cool by today's standards."

"Admirable, in my view," I said, thinking of Jane and me.

Mr. Cooksley gave me a square look. "You've helped a lot. I'll say that. Sometimes takes a stranger to sort you out when you're in shtook."

"If that's right, I'm glad."

"Seems to me, the trouble is his father died while Karl was still a kid. Before he was old enough to rebel."

"Before he was a teenager?"

"Exactly. Before his balls dropped. If he had, rebelled a

bit I mean, kicked over the traces, like most boys do when they're that age, he might have got aback of his father and become his own man."

"Deidentified."

"Is that what it's called?"

"By the developmental psychologists."

"Really? Well, whatever it's called, he never did it."

"From what you say and from what Karl has told me, he loved his father as much as one person can love another. I'm not sure that's such a bad thing."

"However much you love somebody, you should always keep a part of yourself to yourself. Never give it all. You can never be yourself otherwise. And when his father died, Karl felt he'd pretty much died with him. That's what's caused the trouble. He's struggling to find himself. Like who he is. What he is."

I said nothing. We were on touchy ground.

"That's my opinion, anyway," Mr. Cooksley said.

I said, "He's told you he wants to do more sculpting?"

"We talked about it."

"But he wants to go on being a plumber. To keep his feet on the ground, so to speak."

Mr. Cooksley smiled.

"I'm proud of him for that," he said.

"Maybe the sculpting will help him find himself."

"You think so? I can't see it myself. But there's always hope."

When everyone had gone, Mrs. Williamson, Karl and I cleared away the debris and washed up. Then Mrs. W. went off home, leaving Karl and me to return ourselves to normal. But I sensed that in some as-yet-indefinable way the party had caused a change in our friendship.

It was dark by then, and frosty. Icy, in fact, which, sitting in the warmth of my kitchen over final mugs of coffee, neither of us realised.

"That went well," I said.

"Some of it was all right," Karl said.

"Only some? Everybody liked your sculpture."

Karl huffed. "So they said."

"You didn't believe them?"

"Not all of them. Most of them thought it was just about fishing and the fish were the letters to make words."

"You mean they only took it literally?"

"They didn't get it."

"How do you know?"

"Their eyes. They said nice things. But you could tell from their eyes they didn't mean it."

"Give them a chance! People don't always catch on straightaway."

"Maybe."

He drank his coffee.

I said, "You find it hard to take compliments."

He gave me an unyielding look.

"Do I?" he said dismissively.

But I wasn't going to be put off.

"You shy away when you're praised," I said. "You didn't believe them when they said they liked it. Would you have believed them if they'd said they didn't like it?"

"Probably."

"Why?"

"I don't trust people when they're being too nice."

His head went down. I knew better than to press the point.

Silence.

Then, giving me his wary sidelong look, Karl said, "What did you think of Fiorella?"

Ah, I thought, now we're getting to it.

I said, "Not quite what I expected."

"How?"

"Less sure of herself. Perhaps she was nervous."

"Why?"

"Meeting me, perhaps."

"Why would that bother her?"

"Readers often are when they meet a favourite author. They get excited. And often the author doesn't live up to their expectations. At least, I don't think I do. So they end up disappointed. And that makes them more nervous, because they don't know what to say."

"I don't think that was it."

"What then?"

"It might have been."

"You were there as well. She was probably a bit nervous about that."

"Why?"

"Unsure how you'd treat her. Unsure what to say about your sculpture. Three reasons to be nervous. You, me, and your sculpture."

"Maybe."

"So?"

"She was a ladge."

"A ladge?"

"Yes."

"You've lost me."

"A *ladge*. You know."

"No, I don't know."

"A ladge. An embarrassment."

"That's a new one."

"No, it isn't! You should get out more."

"I told you this was a day for telling truths. So she embarrassed you?"

"Yes. You didn't notice?"

"Not particularly."

"The way she trumped around the lads? And the hyper guff about the sculpture?"

"I didn't hear. I saw you talking, but I was talking to your boss at the time."

What I didn't say, because it was so obvious there was no need, is that nothing kills love—and friendship come to that—more quickly than embarrassment.

Trying not to sound too obvious about why, I asked, "What about her friend?" I'd spotted them talking for a lot longer than he and Fiorella spent together.

"Becky? She's OK. I like her. She said some interesting things about sculpture."

"Such as?"

"She asked what got me started. I told her. And she knew about Tucker. William Tucker."

"Really? What a coincidence!"

"She's doing art history. First year at uni. King's College London. She's a year older than Fiorella. Keen on sculpture. She understood what I'm trying to do straightaway. Which Fiorella certainly didn't. I didn't have to tell her. She told me! She's seen a piece by Tucker at the Tate. Very minimal. The work independent of the subject. Getting the richest effect from the simplest means. That's what I'm after. We're going to see it together."

Even his vocabulary had changed: Tucker . . . A piece by . . . Uni . . . Minimal . . . The work independent of, etc. . . . Richest effect from, etc. . . . The Tate.

All in one afternoon's conversation.

The changeful power of instant recognition!

I smiled to myself.

Hello, Becky. Good-bye, Fiorella.

Karl sped on. "She's read a book Tucker wrote about sculpture. Told me some of the stuff in it. Made a lot of sense. She's lending it to me."

"What did she say about yours?"

"She made a good suggestion for how to make it better. As soon as she said it, I could have kicked myself. Should have seen it myself."

"Well, that's OK. You still can."

"Yes. A good thing I didn't have time to fix it."

"So you'll be seeing Becky again."

"She's coming to help me take the piece back home tomorrow. She'll borrow her dad's car, so I won't need to bother you."

Well, I thought, that's a step in the right direction.

But, all the same, isn't jealousy an ugly emotion!

"I'd better push off," Karl said. "Thanks for today."

"I enjoyed it. See you tomorrow."

"Becky's picking me up from work. So we'll be here about six."

It was then we heard the racket in the garden.

TWEN+Y-FIVE

- - - - - - -

I KNEW THEM AT ONCE, EVEN THOUGH THE ONLY LIGHT WAS THE FADED orange blear from the streetlamp some way down on the other side of the road. The four who had jeered. The four from the incident in the pub. The four brain-dead apprentice thugs.

And this time not even the parade-ground authority of ex–warrant officer Cooksley would have stifled their mob-handed intent.

By the time Karl and I were outside and had taken in what was going on, they were ripping apart the rods from the sculpture and flinging them around the garden.

Karl let out a cry of rage and launched himself in rugger-style at the nearest vandal.

Instinctively aware that this was not a wise move, I shouted at him to stop and set off after him, meaning to hold him back. But had taken no more than a couple of

237

strides when one of the rods came flying at me, struck me on the chest so hard that I stumbled, my foot slipped on the icy path, and down I went, cracking my head on the stone wall dividing my garden from my neighbour's.

I came to in a hospital bed an hour or so later. For once, I can't be exact about the time.

What happened next I know only from what I was told by Mrs. Williamson and Karl himself over the next two days, and from the testimony of my next-door neighbour, Gillian, a middle-aged divorced librarian, Tom the publican from the pub up the road, and the police, during the trial of the four offenders in the magistrate's court a couple of months later.

Karl's rugger tackle brought down one of the four, who struggled to get free while yelling to his pals to "get 'im off of me." Karl was sure it was the one he'd had the barney with in the pub. (I learned the names of the four of them from the police after they were arrested. But can't use their names for legal reasons.)

The others came to his aid and hauled Karl to his feet.

But Karl, with his robust and fit 180 pounds in full flood of anger, was not a force to mess with. And though his assailants were the soul of bravery when mob-handed and timidly opposed, their emboozed physique was no match for an enraged Karl. As he twisted out of their grip their flabby condition was no protection against an elbow rammed into the brewer's gut of one, a plumber's fist jabbed into the snozzle of another and a back-footed kick into the groin of the third.

The gutted one bent double, gripping his belly while he chundered the evening's intake onto his feet. The snozzled one staggered back, holding his face in his hands while letting out a sound resembling an alpine yodel. And the groined one fell jackknifed to the ground, knees up and hands gripping himself between his legs, while alternately moaning and sobbing.

This should have been the end of it. But in the time the bout with the threesome was in progress, the one Karl had felled got to his feet, grabbed a rod, and as Karl turned from his demolition job, he thrashed the rod across Karl's left leg just below the knee, sending Karl sprawling to the ground, gasping with pain. He knew at once that his leg was broken and didn't try and stand.

It's anyone's guess whether the gang would have taken the chance to exact vengeance and cause more injury had it not been for Tom the publican, alarmed by the noise, coming to see what was going on. What he didn't know was that Gillian had heard the noise when it started, had got out of bed and looked out of her bedroom window. Seeing the yobs attacking the sculpture she had called the police. And then, when she saw me collapse, had called an ambulance as well.

Tom recognised the foursome only too well from

other episodes in his pub besides the one involving Karl. He would have tried to detain them but when he saw me comatose on the path and Karl shouting that his leg was broken, he decided it was more important to attend to us.

Gillian opened her window and shouted to Tom that she had called the police and an ambulance.

This news galvanised the foursome, distracting them enough from nursing their various bruises to hightail it out of the garden and away up the road.

The rest is straightforward. The police arrived and learned from Karl, Tom and Gillian what had happened and who the perpetrators were. The ambulance arrived moments after the police and carted Karl and me to hospital. Karl phoned his mother while we were on the way. Mrs. W. took a taxi to the hospital. She was the first person I saw when I came to.

Gillian made sure everything was secure in my house and locked up. We have keys to each other's house in case of emergency when one of us is away.

The foursome were rounded up by the police next day, appeared before the magistrates on charges of grievous bodily harm, trespass and destruction of property. They were bound over to keep the peace until their trial came to court two months later. They were found guilty, but because they had no previous convictions, and their snazzy lawyer, paid for by the local councillor father of one of them, argued they had been provoked by Karl attacking them and were only acting in self-defence, they received a telling-off by the magistrate, and were sentenced to twelve months' probation and one hundred hours' community service.

TWENTY-SIX

THERE ISN'T MUCH MORE TO TELL.

As I mentioned, when I came to in the hospital, Mrs. Williamson was at my bedside. I was dazy and remember only that she made sure I was conscious and aware of where I was and what had happened to me but nothing more, before she went off to be with Karl, about whose condition she said nothing and I was still too confused to ask.

Later, a nurse told me I was suffering from concussion and because I'd been unconscious for so long, which was a bad thing, and because of my age, when complications might set in, they needed to keep me under observation for a day or two.

I also needed three stitches in the cut on my head where I had hit the wall, and treatment for a few bruises sustained when I fell down. As it turned out I was perfectly all right and recovered without any ill effects.

It was not until the next day that I heard about Karl.

Mrs. Williamson came to see me around midday, bearing the usual hospital gifts: fruit, flowers, soft drinks.

She asked me how I was before detailing the events of the night before. And only then, when, I suppose, she had assured herself that I was strong enough to bear it, she told me about Karl.

His leg was so badly shattered they had performed an emergency operation, which took four hours to complete, during which the surgeons inserted a metal pin into his tibia and repaired the other bones and muscles as best they could.

His mother had been with him when he regained consciousness that morning, and had only come to me when Karl drifted off to analgesic sleep. The doctors thought the operation had been a success, but they wouldn't know for sure for a few days. Karl was young and strong and fit and was responding well to treatment, so there was, they'd told Mrs. Williamson, no cause for worry and every sign that all would turn out well.

We reassured each other with the usual bromides: he'd pull through, he'd be OK, he was in good hands, everything was being done that could be done.

But our eyes spoke realities to each other, not hopes. We both knew that every operation is a risk, and doctors are always optimistic and put the brightest spin on a prognosis.

As we looked at each other, Mrs. Williamson's eyes filled

with tears, she reached out, took my hand in both of hers and held it tight.

In all she had gone through with Karl in the past year, not once during the trauma of his crisis or the relief of his recovery, not once until now had she touched me intimately.

"I'm sorry!" she said, but held on.

"Don't be," I said. "I'm glad you can."

"It's the sight of him lying there like that. Tubes and drips. His leg. Unconscious. Helpless. And not able to do anything."

"Being there," I said.

"D'you think he knows? When he wasn't conscious, I mean. When he's not awake."

"My wife," I said, "before she died. She was in a coma for a while. I was with her all the time. When she came out of it, she thanked me for staying with her. I asked her, I said, 'You knew?' Yes, she said, she'd known. Not like when she was awake but not like in a dream, either. A different kind of knowing. But she knew. She said she knew she was going. But because I was there, she wanted to come back and say good-bye. She died a few hours later."

Mrs. Williamson let out a deep sigh. "We never know," she said. "We don't know everything about life. Or death, come to that. Do we?"

I said with a "that's life" smile, "No, we don't."

She smiled too and gave a fatalistic shrug.

I said, wanting to give her the cue to go back to her

244

son, "Thanks for coming to see me. And for the gifts. I'm OK. I'm fine. Waited on hand and foot. Having a holiday really."

"I'll come back later," she said.

"Say hello to Karl for me and give him my love."

"I certainly will," she said.

I was sorry to lose her hands.

The day was long. They wanted me to rest and avoid all strenuous activity. They had to be sure the symptoms were clearing up and I didn't need a brain scan. The worst of it was they wouldn't let me read or write because that was supposed to be bad for me too. I realised once more how unbearable life would be if I could never read and write again.

Mrs. Williamson visited briefly that evening. Karl was recovering well. "Sitting up and taking notice," she said. But was still fuzzy from the anaesthetic and the painkillers they were giving him.

She was going home for the night. Would be back tomorrow.

Next day was a day of visits.

Twice from Mrs. Williamson. The first time, happier, livelier, more confident, more like her best self. Karl was doing well.

The second time late that day, less hearty. Karl had

taken a dip. The nurses said it was normal. Postoperative depression. As the anaesthetic wore off the patient was more aware of the pain, more aware of the consequences of what had happened. But Mrs. Williamson felt there was more to it than that. She recognised the signs. Karl had withdrawn into himself, wouldn't talk about what was really bothering him. She was afraid this latest catastrophe might trigger the melancholia again.

Between Mrs. Williamson's visits two others.
The first from Fiorella, in the afternoon.

When I met her at the party, we said only a few words to each other. Not enough for me to gain any sense of what she was really like. People often put on their party persona along with their party clothes, and just as often their persona, like their clothes, is quite the opposite of their everyday self. Which of us would want to be judged by our hair-down hijinks?

Fiorella was certainly got up to kill that day, leaving, as Mr. Cooksley put it, "not much to the imagination," and strutted her stuff to the delight of the rugby youngbloods and the (envious?) scandal of the ancientry. ("I'm glad she's not my daughter," Mr. Cooksley muttered.) I thought at the time, whatever else you could say about Fiorella, one thing was for sure: she did nothing by half.

I say she delighted the youngbloods. But as I discovered later (and report in chapter twenty-four), one youngblood was not impressed—Karl, for whose eyes, I supposed, Fiorella had dolled herself up in her glad rags (if anything as expensive could be called rags) and to capture whose attention she flounced among the lads. Maybe she hoped the flames of jealousy might reignite Karl's interest in her. If so, she badly misread her man.

When Fiorella turned up unexpectedly in the hospital, she was subdued and dressed as soberly as a nun.

Strangely enough, given what she said later, my instant thought was: She's a performer. An actress. Her emails, I saw then, were all performances, voices she was acting out to see how they sounded. So who and what was the real Fiorella?

"Becky told me what happened," Fiorella said with the face of a tragedian. "I thought I'd come and see how you are."

"Very good of you," I said, in the role of the suffering patient. "And to see Karl too, of course," I added, switching to the role of the undeceived.

"Yes," Fiorella said, with a quick change from tragic to coy. "But you mainly."

"Really?" The question was rhetorical, and offered with the smile of disbelief.

"I want to explain."

"What is there to explain?"

"Karl and me."

"What about you and Karl?"

Her expression now was of intended seriousness.

She said, "I won't be seeing him anymore."

This was an announcement that worried me. Not for her sake but for Karl's.

"Oh? When was this decided?"

"Yesterday."

"Yesterday? But Karl was out of it most of yesterday. Did you see him then?"

"No. He doesn't know yet. I was going to tell him today, but it wasn't the right time. He's worse than I thought."

"And when it is the right time, what are you going to tell him?"

"That he isn't my type."

"I see! Well, in fact, I don't see. I'm surprised, after all you wrote in your emails."

"I was wrong. I thought he was, but he isn't."

"And this became clear to you yesterday?"

"Yes."

"And what was it you realised?"

"That I'd been pretending."

"Pretending? Pretending what?"

"Well, for a start, that I didn't mind standing in the cold on the touchline while he played rugby when I'm actually not that keen on rugby, and then not seeing him for hours afterwards while he raved it up with his rugby mates. And pretending I didn't mind sitting under a tree all day while he fished and paid me no attention, when I'm not that keen on fishing or sitting under trees all day. Maybe I wouldn't

have minded the rugby and the fishing if he'd talked to me
about himself. And if he'd paid me more attention. But I
never felt he was really thinking about me. It was always
like there was something else than me on his mind and I
didn't know what it was and he wouldn't tell me. I did try.
That's why I gave him the list of questions. And I thought
if I asked him to write the answers it would be easier for
him. I'm not that keen myself on talking about myself, but
I do like writing about myself and I thought he might be
like that too. Big mistake, as it turned out. But how was I
to know he was dyslexic? He didn't tell me, and neither did
his mother. It might have been different if I'd known. Too
late now, though."

"But you must have known all along, about the rugby
and the fishing?"

"I did. But, like I said, I pretended. To myself, not just
to him. Because physically he is my type. And there is
something about him. Like a mystery, a secret, something
special locked up inside. And I really wanted to know what
it was. And I thought I could kind of, you know, *unlock*
it. And he was keen on me. Very keen. So I thought he'd
let me in if I went along with him. So I did . . . Do you
understand?"

"I think so. But what happened that made everything
clear?"

"When I went to see him in his shed. His workshop.
I wrote to you about it."

"I remember."

"We'd broken it off after . . . the trouble at the camp."

"You'd broken it off, to be accurate."

"Yes, I broke it off. But then I regretted it. I couldn't get him out of my mind. So I thought I'd try again and went to see him. And I told you how I felt like I was being tested. But I didn't know what the test was. Like an exam when you're expected to give the answer to a question you haven't been asked but have to guess."

"I think you're right. You were. Karl is like that. He does test you. He wants to be understood without having to explain."

"I wrote to you about it. And all you wrote back was 'Think artefact.'"

"I did."

"But I couldn't think what you meant."

"No?"

"No. I mean, I guessed you meant it had something to do with the bits of wire I'd seen. But what? I couldn't work it out. You really weren't much help."

"I'm sorry." I lied. I wasn't a bit sorry. If she couldn't work out what I meant, she was right, Karl wasn't her type. More important—which Fiorella didn't seem to have considered so far—Karl knew for sure then, that day in his workshop, that she wasn't his type, either.

"It only came to me what you meant," Fiorella went on, "at the party. You meant the bits of wire had something to do with Karl making something, and Karl was testing me to find out if I understood and what I thought of it."

I nodded.

"And then it was too late."

I nodded again. "You'd missed the moment," I said.

"What d'you mean?"

"Sometimes the course of our lives depends on what we do or don't do in a few seconds, a heartbeat, when we either seize the opportunity, or just miss it. Miss the moment and you never get the chance again."

"That's sad."

"And we never forget and always regret a missed moment."

"Are you talking from experience?"

"I try never to talk from anything else."

She heaved a sigh.

"That isn't all," she said.

"There's something else?"

"Becky."

"Becky?"

"The girl who was with me at the party?"

"I know who you mean. But what about her?"

"I brought her with me for, you know . . . ?"

"Moral support?"

"I was nervous about meeting you and seeing Karl again. And with a lot of other people. I didn't know what to say to him or how he'd treat me."

"And?"

"Well, you must have seen. I'm sure everybody did. How he and Becky got on. I never expected that. I didn't

251

think she was his type at all. She's quiet and studious. A bit of a nerd really. Mad keen on art. To be honest, one reason I asked her was because I thought . . . you know . . . she was . . . safe. But you must have noticed?"

"I did have an inkling."

"Well, she went a bundle on him."

"And Karl?"

"He talked more to her than he's ever talked to me."

"So you decided to cut your losses?"

"I wouldn't put it quite like that!"

"No, sorry. A bit commercial. Blame it on my concussed brain. I'm still not thinking straight."

Another lie. It seemed pretty obvious to me.

"There's just one more thing?"

"Which is?"

"Would you tell Karl for me?"

"Tell him what?"

"That I won't see him again."

I couldn't help laughing.

"Certainly not! You must tell him yourself."

"You wrote those emails for him."

"That was different."

"I don't see how."

"Different or not, I won't make that mistake again. You told me off for doing it, remember?"

"But it's just that I don't want to see him again. I'd say it all wrong. And get upset. And now there's Becky. Who is a friend and I don't want to lose her. And I might if she thinks I'm trying to take Karl from her. I mean, she really is gone on him. She talks about nothing else, which isn't like her at all. I've never heard her talk about a boy for more than about two minutes before. I thought she didn't like boys, to be honest. So you do see, don't you?"

"I see, but sorry, Fiorella. This is something you have to do yourself."

She looked miserable and sat in silence.

For the first time, I felt sorry for her. A performer who hadn't yet found the role she was meant to play. And at the moment, she was failing at every role she tried on. But eventually, she would get it right. She was a trier. My guess is she is one of those people who are so self-confident, and are so well supported at home, and so admired wherever they go, that they can play around, trying roles out, getting them wrong, and bounce back without too much hurt or damage to their egos. The kind of people who always fall on their feet, whatever catastrophes beset them, many of which they cause themselves.

And Karl? He was the opposite of that. Which is why Fiorella found him so fascinating. Fiorella knew without even thinking about it that, give or take the occasional failure, she'd always succeed. What she didn't know was that Karl thought he was nothing else but a failure. (I knew this because it takes one to know one.) This was the secret Fiorella sensed was locked up inside him. And what she didn't know she wanted to know was what it is like to believe you are a failure and that you always will be.

And what neither of them knew, and Karl needed to know, and I'd learned the hard way, was how to turn his belief in himself as a failure into success. Which is what I'd hoped he was about to discover, and which I worried might now be impeded by the calamity after the party.

Fiorella stood up. "Oh well, I'll just have to write to him and tell him."

"Maybe that's best," I said.

She nodded. "Well, then. I'll say good-bye."

"Good-bye, Fiorella. Best of luck to you."

"I'll still read your books."

"Thanks. I need all the readers I can get."

"Get well soon."

As she walked away, I felt better about her. Beneath all the outward show, her tryout performances, there was a good and sensitive person. She'd had a pretty easy life. Then Karl came along, awkward, wary, passionate and withdrawn at the same time, a combination of physical strength and emotional weakness, of certainty and doubt. She wanted to be loved by him but, for the first time in her life, she couldn't quite capture someone with her charm. Whatever gambit she played, Karl answered with an unexpected move, one of which shocked her and almost caused her to give up the game. But she returned because she couldn't bear the thought of failing and hoped to checkmate him by one final desperate move. Now she had retired hurt. And though she couldn't acknowledge it yet, she would be all the better for it.

That evening I was told I could get up next day.

And go home?

The doctor was concerned because there was no one to look after me. So perhaps I should stay another day just to make sure all was well?

I said I felt fine, no dizziness, no headache—both were true.

But I hadn't been on my feet since the "accident." So "let's see how things are tomorrow."

I didn't say it, but I had no intention of staying another day in hospital.

Then Becky arrived.

She was—I keep using the past tense; I ought to say she is—one of those people who, at first sight, look plain, are quiet, unassertive, unmemorable even. But who, when they start to talk and you get to know them, become more and more attractive and impressive, and you see that in fact they are beautiful. Not conventionally beautiful, not celebrity beautiful, but beautiful all through.

"Hi," she said. "I'm Becky. I don't know if you remember me? I was at your party."

"Yes, I remember."

"How are you?"

"Fine, thanks. I'll probably be let out tomorrow."

She smiled.

"Good." And then serious, blushing, "It was awful, what happened."

There as an awkwardness about her that was somehow attractive. I'd noticed as she walked towards me that she had feet of the kind that looked as though they'd trip over themselves and make you smile at the sight.

I said, "You've been to see Karl?"

"I've been with him all day. His mother's with him now."

"How is he?"

"All right, I suppose, given he's had a major operation."

"I wanted to go and see him, but they wouldn't let me up. I will tomorrow."

"I wondered about that. He'd like to see you. He's a bit down. Not because of his leg so much but because of his sculpture. He can't bear what they did to it. It's like they destroyed some of himself . . . He doesn't put it like that. He doesn't say it . . . But I can tell that's what he feels. We've tried to reason with him, his mother and me, but it's like he can't hear."

"Or doesn't want to."

"Yes. I haven't known him long. Well, only since the party. But we got on from the first minute. It was like we'd always known each other. We just *fitted* . . . If you know what I mean?"

"I know exactly."

"We talked about his sculpture. Which I think is terrific, don't you? . . . Very like William Tucker's. Karl said you knew Tucker's work."

"Only what I've seen in photos, apart from the one we saw together."

"Well, we talked about that and what he wants to do, and we were going to London to see some other sculptures that I think might interest him . . . But . . . I'm sorry . . ."

"Don't apologise. I'm interested."

"Well, the thing is . . . You see, I don't know what to say that will make him believe again. I mean, believe he should go on."

"Is that what he's saying? That he won't do any more?"

"Yes."

"No, no, no! That won't do. He must do more."

"He *must*. I agree." The slightly awkward, slightly shy manner had gone. She was suddenly very passionate. "When we talked at the party, I could tell. It's him. Sculpture is *him*. It's what he *is*. What he's *meant* to do. Don't you agree? Don't you?"

So, I thought, behind that quiet exterior there lives a determined mind.

"Yes," I said, "I agree."

"I knew you would. I just felt you would."

"Let me think about what to say. And I'll go to him as soon as they'll allow me tomorrow morning."

"Thanks. Thanks so much."

"No need to thank me. You're the one to be thanked."

"Me. Why?"

"For believing in him."

"I do. But you see, I love him. I haven't known him long. A few hours. But I *know*. I think sometimes important things happened to you in a flash. And sometimes it takes ages. And I know people will say I can't know so soon. But I do."

She said this with such matter-of-fact directness, it was utterly convincing.

"And," she said in the same quiet tone, "if you don't mind me saying so, I think you do too. Love him, I mean."

I was so taken aback I couldn't reply.

Luckily, she went straight on. "There's something else."

I waited, still unable to speak.

"If I tell you this, will you promise you won't tell anyone else? No one at all."

"Is it about Karl?"

"Yes."

"Is it bad news?"

"Yes."

"All right. I promise."

"I know one of the nurses on Karl's ward. We went to school together and have stayed friends. She shouldn't have told me but thought I ought to know. She was at a meeting with the ward staff and the surgeon who operated on Karl. The surgeon said Karl would never play rugby again. It would be too risky because of his leg. But they agreed not to tell Karl or anyone else until he's fit again and strong enough to cope with it."

We stared at each other, too upset for words.

All of a sudden, I couldn't bear lying down. My heart was pounding. I had to sit up. I struggled with the bedclothes, pulling them off, and pushed myself up so that I could sit on the edge of the bed.

Becky sat beside me, an arm round my shoulders.

Neither of us said anything.

When I'd caught my breath and my heart had calmed down, I said, "That's not good news."

"The reason I wanted you to know is so you'll see why it's more important than ever we get Karl's mind back on his sculpture."

"Yes, yes, I understand."

"He has to start sculpting again before they tell him."

"You're right. And you did right to tell me. Thanks."

"Between us, and with his mother's help, it'll be OK. Won't it? Don't you think?"

"Yes, yes. He'll still be able to fish. And once he's sculpting and working again, it'll be OK."

"Are you OK?"

"Yes, yes. I'm all right. It was just a shock."

"What about I come to you tomorrow morning and take you to Karl and then leave you together?"

"Good idea. They are being a bit sticky about letting me out tomorrow. No one to keep an eye on me at home, and my age. All that sort of nonsense."

"I see. Well, if they won't let you walk, I'll take you there in a wheelchair!"

I laughed.

"Oh God! Not a wheelchair!"

"I'm only joking."

"Unfortunately, Becky, all too often a joke tells the truth."

She stood up.

"I'd better go. It's nearly chucking-out time and I want to say good night to Karl."

"Go, go. And good night to you."

"I hope you sleep well."

"Till tomorrow."

"Till tomorrow."

She walked away down the ward and out of sight. And all I could think was how lucky she and Karl were to find each other.

Twenty-Seven

CUSSED. PERVERSE. OBSTINATE. SELF-WILLED. BLOODY-minded. Stubborn. Obdurate. Pigheaded. Intransigent. Contumacious . . .

I muttered to myself all the words I could think of that named my reaction to being woken in my hospital bed at six thirty.

I'm always awake at home by that time and usually up by seven. So why resent it in hospital? Because it was required by "them." Because I didn't decide for myself; "they" imposed it on me.

Was I always so bolshy, so obstreperous, so unaccommodating?

I smiled as I remembered how at school I wouldn't read the set books but only other books by the same author or on the same subject instead. And then have to force my grumbling self to mug up the set book at the last minute.

How far back in my life could I trace this intransigence? I remember as a very small boy refusing to eat what my mother put in front of me, and guzzling whatever she didn't want me to eat.

"You've always gone against the grain," my mother once said in exasperation.

I was up, abluted, dressed, and sitting impatiently in the chair beside my bed, plotting how I'd escape if "they" wouldn't let me go by midday, when a nurse hove into view with Mrs. Williamson and Becky, both grinning widely. With a wheelchair!

"Your friends have come to take you home," the nurse said in that cheery way they have. "They've promised to look after you. And we need your bed for a more deserving case."

Mrs. Williamson winked. Becky, behind the nurse's back, put a finger across her lips.

I perspired with gratitude.

And we were out of there in five minutes flat, me reluctantly in the wheelchair—but I'd have put up with anything no matter how humiliating in order to escape.

"How did you do it?" I asked, when we were safely on our way down one of those cubular, vinyl-tiled, antiseptic hospital corridors that seem designed to make you feel ill whether you are or not.

"With a little help from Becky's friend," Mrs. Williamson said, "and as the nurse said, by promising to look after you till you're fully recovered."

"And how do you plan to do that, when you live three miles from my house?"

"We'll talk about that later," Mrs. W. said. "The first thing we have to do is see Karl."

"But it isn't visiting hours yet," I said.

"Mothers have their ways," Mrs. W. said.

"I've met your ways before," I said. "You are a finagling woman."

"You watch your language," Mrs. W. said. "We're taking you to Karl, and leaving you with him for half an hour. That's all you are allowed. Becky and I will have coffee in the café, if you can call it coffee, and we'll fetch you when the time's up and take you home in Becky's father's car. Then Becky will come back to be with Karl while I settle you at home. Understood?"

"Grief!" I said. "You *are* managerial today."

"Stop complaining," Becky said.

"It's the effect hospitals have on me," I said.

"It's the disinfectant," Becky said. "Makes you feel they are about to do something surgical to you. Or it does me, anyway."

"Have they said when Karl can go home?" I asked.

"Not yet," Mrs. W. said.

Becky gave me a look that meant "Don't say any more."

Hospitals are places where we suffer private pain in public. No wonder operations are performed in rooms called theatres. At the same time, they are a kind of prison, which is why the rooms where patients are herded together are called wards. And the nurses, if the one who had just chucked me out was anything to go by, might as well be called warders. (Unless, of course, you have lavish amounts of money and then, as always, everything is different.)

Karl, who hated being on show at the best of times, did indeed look like a prisoner, shackled to his bed by a contraption that suspended his encased leg upstretched in the air as if he'd tried to kick a ball while lying on his back and had got stuck.

His face was a picture of brooding dejection. I remember thinking as I approached his bed: It's not his leg that's making him ill, it's being in hospital.

Mrs. W. and Becky left me by his bedside. We said nothing to each other. But from the moment he saw me he never took his eyes from mine, and that was enough communication between us, knowing each other as we did now.

His eyes said, "Get me out of here."

"They kept me in bed till this morning," I said when it was time to speak.

"Your mother and Becky are taking me home," I said. "They'll come straight back when they've settled me in."

"You're OK?" Karl asked.

"I'm fine," I said. "Concussed. They wanted to be sure it wasn't dangerous. My age and all that guff."

"We'll get you out of here as soon as we can," I said. "You're going to be all right."

"How do you know?" Karl said.

"Medically, you mean? I don't. But you're fit and young and they say they've fixed your leg up good and proper."

"So who does know?" Karl said.

"The doctors. What do they say?"

"That I'll be OK."

"There you are then."

"But I don't trust them."

"Why not?"

"The way they say it. And the way they look at each other and the nurses when they're talking to me. I think they're lying."

"What about your mother? You trust her, don't you?"

"She'll tell me the good news but not the bad. Not while I'm in here. In case I go off the rails again."

"So you feel you can't trust anybody?"

He gave me the hint of a smile.

"What is . . ."

"Is!"

The hint broadened into an actual smile.

"Let's talk about something else," I said. "They won't let me stay long."

"Like what?"

"After the party you said you'd thought of how to make the sculpture better."

He looked away for the first time.

"I'm not doing it again," he said.

"Why not?"

"They'll only smash it up again."

"If they do, you'll make another."

"Oh, thanks!"

"But I don't think they will."

"Why not?"

"That sort get bored very easily. No stamina."

"But what's the use!"

"Doing it. The use is *doing it.*"

"So some dickhead can smash it up."

"That's the reason for doing it again."

"For it to be smashed up? Talk sense!"

"You want the world to be left to the dickheads?"

"Course not!"

"Then you're going the right way about it."

"Me! I'm not doing anything."

"Exactly."

"Exactly *what?*"

"You know why they smashed it up?"

"For fun. For laughs. I don't know."

"Because it threatens them."

"Threatens them? How?"

"Because they don't understand it."

"Neither did most of the people at the party."

"Not the way you wanted them to. But they didn't smash it up."

"Only because they know me."

"Give them a bit more credit than that."

"All right, so they didn't understand it, but they didn't smash it up. So what?"

"They didn't understand it, but they were trying to. They wanted to. That's the difference between them and the dickheads who did smash it up."

He shifted in the bed, trying to sit up more. Winced with the pain the movement caused in his leg.

I said, "I had a chat with your boss at the party."

"And?"

"You've known him a long time, I gathered."

"Since I was born. He was my dad's best friend."

"Did he tell you what he thought?"

"Not his cup of tea."

"Anything else?"

"It was well made."

"Nothing more?"

"No, why?"

"He didn't tell you he was glad you'd made it?"

"No."

"And how proud your father would have been?"

Karl gave me a suspicious look.

"He said that?"

"He did."

"Really?"

"Really."

He turned away.

Then, muttering: "So you're saying the dickheads

smashed it up because they didn't understand it and didn't want to."

"Exactly. And they smashed it up to try and get rid of it. To feel they had won."

He looked at me again. Now his eyes were lively again.

"I'll bet," he said with a grin. "A lot more dickheads around than people who don't understand but want to."

"There are always more destroyers of what you are trying to do than there are people who are on our side."

"Which means they'll always win."

"Only if you stop making. For one thing, the dickheads never manage to smash everything. And for another thing, if you, and the people like you, the true artists, keep on making, the philistines can't smash up everything. There may be fewer of you. *Of us.* But we win in the end."

Silence.

"And even if we don't," I went on after a moment. "Even if they smash everything we make, it doesn't matter, because in making it we give pleasure to people who love us, people who admire us, people who *try* to understand. Like your boss. And your mother . . . And Becky . . . And Fiorella too, you know, whatever you might think about her now."

Another silence. But I could feel his mood shifting.

I took from my pocket the little stone he gave me after we'd built the cairn.

"Remember this?" I said, holding it out in the palm of my hand for him to see.

He glanced at it and turned away again.

"Course. I found it in the river."

"You gave it to me."

"Yes."

"Why?"

"Don't know. I thought you'd like it."

"Only that? We saw a lot of stones that day. Why give me this one?"

"No idea. It just seemed different. I hadn't seen anything like it before."

"What d'you think it is?"

He gave me a huffing look. "A stone with a hole in it."

I laughed out loud.

"What's so funny?"

"You are! You're the one complaining that people don't understand what you're trying to do, but when I show you this, all you can say is it's a stone with a hole in it."

"Get to the point."

"OK. I'll admit, at first, I thought it was just a stone with a hole in it. I kept it on me all the time, because you gave it to me and I valued it for that. I've looked at it a lot. Have a good look at it yourself."

He took it from me, turned it over and over, looked closely at it.

"What d'you think now?"

He was puzzled.

"Dunno."

"D'you think it's just a little stone that got like that naturally. Smooth and perfectly round, and the hole dead centre?"

"Could have done."

"But you're not sure?"

"No. It feels . . ."

"What?"

"That it was made like that."

"Exactly the conclusion I came to. So I did some research."

He eyed me, knowing now I had a surprise in store.

"And?"

"I suspect it's a marriage stone."

"A what?"

"A marriage stone. You know how we give rings when we marry? Well, I think this is a very old version of that. Prehistoric, probably. Thousands of years old. Made by a man to give to the woman who was his wife. She probably hung it round her neck."

"You're not kidding me?"

"No, no. I can't be sure. But I asked someone who's an expert on that kind of stuff and he told me that's what it could be."

He looked at the stone again. Pushed his little finger through the hole, and showed it to me as if it were a ring, and laughed.

As I did too.

"A made thing," I said. "And the man who made it doesn't

have a headache anymore, that's for sure. But now we have it. And even now, thousands of years after it was made, it still gives us pleasure. But more than that, when you picked it out of the river you knew, you knew instinctively, it was something different, something special. And you gave it to me. Why? Not just because you thought I'd like it."

He shook his head.

"Level with me," I said.

"All right! OK! A kind of thank-you."

"Which you were too upset that day to say?"

"Probably."

"Which I knew at the time and appreciated. You didn't need to say it. The stone said it better. Just like I imagine it said more to the lover of the man who made it than he could say in words."

He looked at me hard.

"You needn't go on," he said. "I get the point."

"Exactly. No need to say it. But seeing it's a marriage stone, I think you'd better have it back and keep it for the right person on the right occasion, don't you?"

He laughed. "I'll find something else to give you instead."

"You don't have to. You've already given it to me. It's in my front garden. In pieces, yes, but ready to be put back together. And even better than before."

He nodded and looked away, back to the little stone, which he fingered in his hand.

We were silent again.

Until I said, "Becky came to see me. She's quite something."

He nodded.

"Studies art history."

He nodded.

"I'll tell you what. Ask her about the oldest sculptures in the world and where they are. And then ask yourself how they've survived, just like that marriage stone, for thousands of years, if it's true that the dickheads always win."

Silence again.

Becky and Mrs. W. arrived at the door of the ward.

"I've got to go," I said. "But you know what?"

"What?" Karl said, full face to me again.

"This talk about giving up, and not making any more sculpture, it's not you talking."

"Who, then?"

"Your leg."

He smiled, full and bright, his eyes alive again.

"I'll be back this evening," I said.

I got up and turned to go.

"When you come . . . ," he said.

I turned to face him.

"Yes?"

"Bring some paper and a pencil, will you?"

"Anything else?" I said.

"Some of that wire I use, if you have any."

"No problem," I said.

On the way home we stopped at the nearest supermarket and stocked up with food for me and for Mrs. W.

I didn't let on that I suddenly felt physically weak doing even this undemanding chore. Maybe, I thought, the docs and nurses were right about me being careful for a few days.

Back home, the rods from the sculpture were still scattered around the garden. A forlorn sight. As soon as we had opened up the house, switched on the heating and checked that all was well, Becky collected the pieces of rod and stored them in the garage.

While she was doing that, Mrs. W. prepared a pan of soup, ready for me to heat up at lunchtime.

The first thing I wanted before anything else was a shower. Why is it that hospitals, which are meant to be astringently clean, make you feel grubby and sticky?

Mrs. W. insisted on waiting till I was dressed in clean clothes before she allowed Becky to drive her to her own house, where she wanted to pick up some things for Karl. They both insisted they would call to see me again later, for which I was grateful. I felt wobbly and vulnerable, perhaps unconsciously fearing I might fall down and damage myself again.

When they'd gone, I toured the house, relieved to be among my own things in my own place.

I sat in the reading chair in my workroom. But didn't read. I wanted to rest, breathe myself in again, so to speak.

Didn't want to lie down. I'd had enough of that in hospital.

I thought of everything that had happened in the last few days. And this extended, back and forth, over the events since Karl first came to see me.

And I knew it was time.

I moved to my desk. The desk on which I've written all my books. I've never been able to write them anywhere else.

You must go on making, I'd told Karl.
You can't let the philistines destroy you.

What was true for Karl was true for me.
You mustn't allow even death to destroy you.
And it can't if you live in what you make.

I looked at the photo of Jane, which has always stood on my desk. And I knew what she would say.
If you can't do it for it for yourself, do it for me.

I took from my drawer a new refill pad made of recycled paper, with faint narrow ruled lines and four holes in the margin for filing. I've always used them for drafting my books.
I took a new 2B pencil. The kind I always use.

I wrote the date and time at the top of the page. I always do when I start a day's work.

And began.

"Could I talk to you?"

"Why?"

THIS BOOK WAS DESIGNED

by Robyn Ng and art directed by Chad W. Beckerman. The text is set in 12-point Adobe Garamond, a typeface based on those created in the sixteenth century by Claude Garamond. Garamond modeled his typefaces on ones created by Venetian printers at the end of the fifteenth century. The modern version used in this book was designed by Robert Slimbach, who studied Garamond's historic typefaces at the Plantin-Moretus Museum in Antwerp, Belgium. The display type is Hannah.

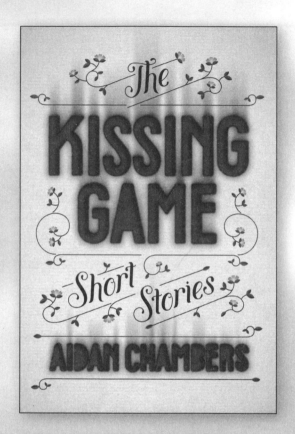